S0-ACU-475

THE ROAD
TO
RATENBURG

~THE ROAD TO~ RATENBURG

Joy Cowley

Illustrations by
Gavin Bishop

GECKO PRESS

*For Aimee Demers, a teacher who brings a love
of reading to children, and for her beautiful
daughter Calli, who shares that love. JC*

CONTENTS

CHAPTER ONE

AN ACT OF REMARKABLE DESTRUCTION

Dear Friend,

Please allow me, Spinnaker Rat of the Ship rat clan, to give you a full account of an extraordinary journey undertaken by one rat family. I beg you, do not allow our story to bring you fear. This book has in it much danger and some moments of sheer terror, but all of it is history, meaning it is in the past and therefore of no threat to you.

1

I suggest, however, that it not be read to furry youngsters at bedtime, or to the elderly who still have nightmares about cats and dogs and wicked traps.

First, let me tell you about the humming-bean abode where we once lived in a crowded basement. The name "humming bean" came from one of our young rats, who couldn't make sense of "human being", and thereafter my wife and I used humming bean to describe the two-legged creatures who lived in layers of nests in our apartment building—although why the nests were called *apart*-ments, when they were so close together, always puzzled me.

The air vents from floor to floor were highways for the rat families who occupied our basement. At night we would run past each other, whispering the latest food news. "Bacon rinds, third den, fourth floor." "Big den top floor left out a bowl of peanuts, and their cat is at the vet." Once, a humming bean left a large cake in a plastic bag outside one of the doors on the ground floor. Thin plastic! I tell you, not a crumb survived the night.

My darling wife Retsina is fond of Mediterranean food, since her family lived at the back of a Greek restaurant. In the apartment building, she would brush her whiskers against my ear and sigh, "Oh, Spinnaker! What I would give for some black olives or a taste of lamb souvlaki!" Then our four children, Alpha, Beta, Gamma and Delta, would start squeaking. "Papa! Go around the television rooms! See if there's any popcorn!"

As you will assume, I was the proud hunter and gatherer, and most nights I ran back and forth with tasty morsels for my family. Although the humming beans were enemies in the same class as cats, dogs and hawks, they also provided food for us, and I was cautiously grateful—that is, until the great migration.

None of us knew why the humming beans left the building, taking their furniture with them. One by one the levels emptied and our sources of nutrition dried up. Our basement neighbour Roger said the people were all on summer vacation and would soon be back with sacks of food. I believed that no more than I believed his full name was Jolly Roger and that he was descended from a clan of Pirate rats. All that "Ahoy, me hearties!" and "Shiver me timbers!" didn't fool me for a moment. He was an actor, was Roger—most likely a Theatre rat from some insignificant hole at the back of a stage.

One morning Roger announced, "They have returned!" For a moment, I thought he was right as doors slammed and heavy feet echoed on the stairs. These humming beans, however, were not the ones who had left. They wore orange coat-skins and carried barrels that definitely did not smell of food. We assumed the round things were new furnishings for the dens.

When the heavy feet marched down to the basement, we crept back to our nests. Retsina and I, with our four children, lived behind the water pipes in a nest made out of cloth borrowed from the laundry room. Most comfortable it was, too. Peering between the pipes, we saw the barrels set up around the basement and strung together with strands of wire. It was all very curious. Even Jolly Roger, who made up stories because he didn't like saying "I don't know", was silent. No one knew what the barrels meant.

After the men left, Retsina sniffed a barrel. "Totally inedible!" she said. "My dear Spinnaker, there's not a scrap of food in this building. Every rat in their right mind has left! I'm going to the Greek restaurant. I'll take the children with me and we'll drag back enough food to last two days."

I felt uneasy. I should tell you, dear friends, that I have a slight nervous disorder inherited from my father, Mizzen Rat. When danger is around the corner, my whiskers twitch. They were twitching now. "Dear wife, don't go. I am the provider. Be patient. I'll go to the bin at the back of the supermarket."

"No, Spinnaker!" Retsina was stubborn in her charming way. She snuggled close and licked the thin fur behind my ear. "Wouldn't you like some baklava? Pastry with ground nuts, honey and rose water?"

4

My whiskers were still trembling but I let her go with the children. After all, she knew the road to the Greek restaurant so well that she could get there with her eyes shut, and there were no cats or dogs on the way. But the nervous unease was still with me, so I went up to the ground floor where the orange-skinned humming beans had exited the building, and that's where I found a treasure on the floor. In a crumpled paper bag was a fresh brown crust with a delicious smear of peanut butter. I picked it up between my teeth, tasting but not biting, and took it back to the basement. If my darling wife and children found nothing outside the restaurant, they would not go hungry.

As luck would have it, Jolly Roger crossed my path. "What have you got there, old shipmate?" he asked.

To answer, I needed to drop the crust of bread. "I found it near the front door."

He sniffed it. "You'll not be wanting all that, will you?"

I was so shocked by his impudence that I was slow to answer. As fast as a blink, he had the crust between his thieving paws. "I'll pay you back when my ship comes in!" he cried, then he flicked the bread into the air, caught it between his teeth and ran off.

Now there is something you should know about me. I take pride in being patient, considerate and polite, but when my family is threatened, those virtues disappear.

My fur was bristling with fury! Retsina and our four young ones had left the building to look for food. I, on the other hand, had found a crust of fresh bread for them. Now Roger had pirated it. I screeched at him and tried to bite his tail, but he was much too speedy. He ran through the basement to the outside drain, and with the bread still between his teeth, he scampered down the road.

I chased after him, squeaking, and it was my anger that saved my life. No sooner had we reached the corner of the street than the sky filled with thunder and the ground wobbled beneath our feet, as though the pavement, too, was shaking with rage. The thunder grew louder. I thought the world was breaking apart. I turned and saw our apartment building fall down on itself and a great cloud of dust billow up the street. Roger dropped the bread crust and ran. I didn't pick it up, but ran also, as the dust cloud rolled in our direction. I followed Roger into an alleyway and we hid behind some crates containing empty bottles. The cloud reached into the entrance of the alleyway, feeling for us, but it didn't come far. We crouched behind the crates, shaking, waiting for the dust to settle.

After all that noise, the quiet that filled our ears made us think that the world had ceased to exist. We crept out of the alleyway and, to tell the truth, I completely forgot about the bread. The tall apartment building of many dens had gone, and where it had once blocked the sun there was now blue sky. All that was left was a hill of rubble, stones and bricks, through which could be seen a bit of a door, a twisted window.

"Shiver me timbers!" said Roger. "Saved by a crust of bread!"

Far from being angry, I was now very grateful. If he hadn't stolen my family's meal, and I hadn't chased him, we'd both have been crushed under all those stones. I realised that maybe some rats had not been so fortunate. I shivered when I thought of those who had not got away. Now I knew why my whiskers had twitched!

"Demolition," said Roger. "Those barrels were bombs. You know, like cannon! Like torpedoes! Boom, boom! Smithereens!"

I assured him that I did know about explosives.

"No, you didn't! You thought those barrels were furniture!"

I refused to argue with him. Now the most important thing was to find my family and tell them I was safe.

Retsina and the little ones had gone towards the Greek restaurant, but when they heard the thunder, they'd turned back. They feared I had been in the building and had run through the cloud of dust so that their fur was powdered grey. My dear wife was trembling. She sprang at me, licking my face with such tenderness that I was both pleased and embarrassed. "You're safe!" she sobbed.

"I saved him," Roger announced. "Otherwise he'd be as flat as ship's biscuit." He sidled up to her, presenting his cheek to be licked.

Retsina looked at me and I had to nod. "It's true." So she gave him a quick lick near his ear, and then came back to me, her paws kneading me as though she could not believe I was truly alive. Not only that, but our four beautiful children were leaping at me, squeaking, "Papa! Papa!" the dust falling off their coats.

Perhaps I should tell you more about our ratlets. They are all the same age, of course. Retsina is not sure which was born first because they all came rather quickly, and she had her eyes closed. I came home to find four pink babies as bald as peanuts and blind, happily drinking from their mother. She had already named them. Her own name was that of a traditional Greek wine, but she wanted something classical for her children, and what could be more elegant than the first four letters of the Greek alphabet?

The biggest ratlet, a daughter, is Alpha and she takes after my side of the family. She loves adventure and longs to be a Ship rat like my father and those before him. Beta, also female, is small and chubby and has her mother's fondness for fine food. She is a kindly little thing, tender-hearted, and will give sad squeaks if someone is hurt. Then come our sons. Gamma can't sit still. He is sporty and restless, very fast, good at climbing, the one in the family who can scuttle up a wall to reach a slice of salami on a high shelf. Of all four, Delta is the most practical. He has a good sense of direction and is skilled at problem solving. It is Delta who has inherited my concern for family.

When we are together we feel that we can survive anything. That day we stared at the wrecked building and were glad, so very glad, that we were all safe. We had each other. Our home was gone, but we would find somewhere else.

I looked up and saw Jolly Roger bouncing about, seeking attention. "I saved him!" he cried. "If it wasn't for me he'd be squished and squashed."

Our charming little Beta ran to him. "Thank you, Uncle Roger, for saving our papa."

He patted her on her head. "Think nothing of it, small one." He looked at Retsina and me. "Well, me hearties, where do we go now?"

Retsina rolled her eyes, but we both knew we would not easily be rid of Jolly Roger, especially now that he considered himself my rescuer. I said, "Tonight we can go back to the end of the alley. The space behind those crates is too narrow for stray cats. We'll be safe there."

None of us had eaten that day but we were all too disturbed to worry about food. The corner of the alley smelled of moss, sour milk and ancient cat pee, but no cat would be able to shift the heavy crates to reach us. We made ourselves as comfortable as we could, although the night was cold and damp. Looking up at the sky was like gazing from a hole in the ground, for around us were towering apartments. Above the only building with a low roof, I saw a familiar light.

I nudged Retsina. "Look! Our star!"

Jolly Roger, at the end of the line behind Gamma, raised his head. "Where?"

"See?" Retsina pointed with her delicate nose. "Up there. The brightest one."

"That's not a star," snorted Roger. "That's the planet Venus."

"It's our family star," my wife said firmly.

"A planet isn't a star!" argued Roger. "All Pirate rats know the planet of Venus. How else do you think we navigate?"

I wanted to remind him that Pirate rats were stow-aways on pirate ships and they didn't navigate, but I was too tired to take part in one of his silly discussions. It was Alpha, always curious, who asked, "Planet or star? Which is it?"

"Planet!" said Roger.

Retsina ignored him. She said to Alpha, "We call it a star because it belongs to us."

"How do we know, Mama?" Alpha snuggled closer. "Who said it was ours?"

Retsina put a paw over her. "You know your letters, Alpha. Tell me, how do you spell star backwards?"

"Oh," whispered Alpha. "Now I remember."

I fully expected Jolly Roger to begin another argument, but he'd gone to sleep, and a short time later he was snoring through his front teeth. Soon all the ratlets were closing their eyes, and only my wife and I were gazing at the sky where our star hung, promising a bright future. I put my nose near Retsina's ear. "Tomorrow we find a new home. Where does my darling want to make our nest? In the city? The country? Perhaps by the sea?"

She was quiet for a moment, then she whispered, "Do you think we should go to Ratenburg?"

CHAPTER TWO

A LONG AND DIFFICULT JOURNEY IS PLANNED

Here, a small hesitation may be necessary, dear friend. Most rats know about Ratenburg but for other creatures the name could be unfamiliar. Let me tell you the history of the beautiful city of Ratenburg, built exclusively for rats. Its founder was a humming bean who suffered none of the ratophobia typical of his kind. He actually admired and respected all rats. He lived in ancient times, a piper who wore a two-coloured skin, and was asked by the Lord Mayor of Hamelin to rid the town of its rat population. Ever since, humming beans have told the story that the piper led the rats to a river where they all drowned, but believe me, that is ratist propaganda. This man was definitely on the side of rats, so our ancestors were taken to a valley between two mountains where a city of tunnels and nests had been built.

Ratenburg! Oh, what a glorious place! Descriptions of its splendour had come down through history. Walls of marble lined with silk! Granaries full of corn and peas, dairies stocked with cream, butter and large round cheeses! Storehouses of German sausages and French pastries! In Ratenburg it is not necessary to hide by day and hunt by night, because there are no enemies in the region: cats, traps, hawks, dogs are unknown and the only humming bean ever to set two feet in that valley was the friendly piper of ancient times.

So why, you ask, don't all rats migrate to Ratenburg? Ah, how we wished it were that easy. Although most of us knew the approximate direction, no maps were available. Those who left the humming-bean cities to travel to Ratenburg never returned so we didn't know if they were living in splendid safety. Possibly they had become lost and had settled elsewhere or, worse still, had fallen prey to predators. That was my great fear for my family. What evils lay hidden on the road? What creatures waited to make a meal of unsuspecting rats?

All this Retsina and I had discussed many times, and

although I was surprised that she should mention it again, I was too tired to talk with any degree of seriousness.

As uncomfortable as we were, we slept all night with the exhaustion of a family that had just escaped death.

Early morning. It was time to go. We needed to get off the streets before the humming beans began walking their ferocious dogs.

"The train station," suggested Retsina. "That will be a good place for us."

I agreed that the railway yards offered a variety of shelter. They were also quite close. But Roger was not enthusiastic. "Those Railway rats are a fierce lot," he said. "They don't like intruders. I heard they dipped a City rat in a pot of tar and then stuck train tickets all over him. I vote we go somewhere safe."

Retsina sniffed. "I thought Pirate rats were unafraid."

"I'm considering your young ones," Roger said.

It seemed to me that this was an admirable time to be rid of Jolly Roger. "We're going to the train station," I told him. "I suggest you find somewhere else that suits you."

He grunted and grumbled, "Not likely, shipmate. I'll come with you. You might need my protection."

To make a long story short, we set off in the half dark, Retsina leading the way for our ratlets, and I at the rear to guard them against any following cat. Cats strike first with their claws, but an agile rat can bite a soft paw pad, and believe me, a rat's teeth are as sharp as any cat's. I have made many a foul feline yelp and flee on three legs. But what of Jolly Roger? He had tucked himself between Alpha and me and was jittery with fear as we ran along the gutter of the main street. There were only a few humming beans on the pavement. The rest were in vehicles with headlights that stared straight ahead and did not swivel.

As for us, we saw no cats, no dogs. My only concern was Gamma, our athletic son, who could not resist doing double somersaults over the drains. He laughed at my warnings, but if he had fallen down the gratings, we would have attracted attention.

Without too much bother, we arrived at the train station. The parking area was already full of cars, and it was easy to find one that had turned cold. In my young and foolish days I hid under a car that had a warm and throbbing engine. You may imagine my embarrassment when it drove away, leaving me exposed. One humming bean jumped into the arms of another, screaming, "A rat! A rat!" I am accustomed to ratophobia but the shrillness paralysed me. It was only when another humming bean lifted his foot that I realised I was in danger. I ran before the life was stamped out of me.

But I digress, dear friend. There we were, crouched under a car, staring at the bright lights of a building full of humming beans. Almost immediately, we felt a trembling in the concrete beneath us. My heart stopped, remembering yesterday, and Roger squeaked, "Bombs!" But as the ground-shake grew into noise, we realised it was an approaching train. We heard the blast of its whistle at the crossings and the engine came slowly into the station. I crept forward until I could see it, a long row of lights in carriage windows. Humming beans flocked to it. The train was like a great snake that devoured a crowd and then slithered away.

Now the sky was getting light. We needed to find a hiding place before sun-up. Roger said, "There's long grass on the other side of the tracks."

"No," said Retsina. "It's much safer under the station."

"How do we get there, Mama?" asked Delta.

He had a point. With more humming beans arriving for the next train, we could not stroll casually about the place in growing daylight.

My wife smiled. "I know a way in. Follow me."

She led us around the perimeter of the car park, where we were almost hidden by weeds and paper rubbish. In one corner, near the platform, was a drain with wide gratings, and, inside the drain, a plastic pipe. "That pipe goes under the train station," she said.

"You're squeaking mad!" cried Roger. "Do you know how many rats have been drowned trying to negotiate a water pipe? Shiver me timbers! Are you trying to put us all at risk?"

She looked coldly at him. "This pipe is always dry." Then she gathered our ratlets around her and explained. "In the train stations there are poo and pee rooms for humming beans, who call them bathrooms. Afterwards, they wash their paws in big white dishes, but sometimes the dishes overflow, so there are drains in the floor to take away the water."

"And this is the drain pipe," said Delta. "The question is, how often do the dishes overflow?"

"Hardly ever. If they did, the water would go under the station. That's because the Railway rats have chewed off the joint in the drain pipe. This part is always dry. The Railway rats have made it the main road to their dens."

I stared at her. My Retsina is a rat full of surprises. "How do you know all this?"

She put her cheek against mine. "Trust me, my dear Spinnaker." With that, she swung herself between the bars of the grating and held out her paws to catch our little ones.

The pipe was dark and long, and a faint smell of foreign rats mixed with the warmth of our breath. The sound of claws on the plastic was so loud that I guessed the Railway rats would hear us coming. If Roger was right,

and the cousins were hostile, we could be in grave trouble at the other end. I wished I had been first in line, and not Retsina, who was proceeding at such a pace that she was clearly unaware of danger. Her information regarding the chewed-off joint in the pipe was correct. The last length of plastic, hanging loose under the station, swayed as we went through. I saw a circle of dull grey. Beta, in front of me, dropped over the edge and then I was looking at the basement beneath the station. It covered a large area. There were small ventilation grilles around the outside walls, so there was some light in the place, and I saw rats, dozens of them. They looked at us with eyes that were far from friendly.

Retsina had our ratlets around her and was speaking to a big rat with grey whiskers. "I want to talk to Signal," she said.

"Signal ain't here," the grey whiskers replied. "You shouldn't be here, either. You know what we do to burglars? We bite their blinkin' tails off."

At that, I jumped down from the pipe and stood in front of Retsina. "You try it, you old grey mongrel, and it'll be the last thing you do!"

Retsina pushed me aside. "It's all right, Spinnaker." She stepped towards the big rat. "You don't mean any of it, do you, Shunter?"

He peered at her. "Who told you my name?"

"I have to talk to Signal," she said. "When will he return?"

The old rat's mouth quivered as he tried to remember. "You—you—"

"That's right." She smiled. "I'm Retsina. This is my husband, Spinnaker, and these are our young—Beta, Delta, Gamma and Alpha."

He grunted. "You gave your kids weird names."

"Greek," she said.

"Oh yeah, I got it now. You're the furry little thing from the Acropolis restaurant. You've changed."

"So have you, Shunter. I'll ask you again, when will Signal be back?"

"Dunno. He's out on a bin raid. What do you want to see him for?"

"We're taking our family to Ratenburg. Signal always said the best way to start was by train."

There was a movement and a murmuring among the Railway rats, and I sensed a change in the way they regarded us. I felt it appropriate to offer greetings.

"We don't wish to disturb you," I said politely, "but we do need shelter until nightfall. Yesterday we were made homeless when our building was destroyed by an explosion."

Again, the rats shifted and squeaked, and Shunter said, "We heard about that. Your name's Spinnaker—you were a Ship rat then?"

"My father was. He came from a long line of the marine clan."

"Me too!" cried a voice behind me, and Jolly Roger jumped down from the pipe. He had been waiting to see what kind of reception we got, and if there had been a fight, I'm sure he would have turned tail and fled back down the pipe. Now he stood beside me and announced, "I'm Roger. I'm a friend."

"Ship communication?" asked Shunter.

Jolly Roger looked blank.

"Roger as in message finished, over and out," said Shunter.

"Oh. Oh, yeah. Right."

Shunter turned to the other rats. "We're all transport related, so what do you think? I say we offer them hospitality until nightfall."

Murmurs of agreement went through the colony, and everyone relaxed. Shunter took us to a corner of the basement where a nest had been made of straw and torn paper, and told us to wait there until Signal returned. Some of the other rats came around to talk about the demolition of our building. They had all heard what had happened and wanted to know the cause. Roger was glad to have an audience, and what he didn't know he made up. The crust of bread disappeared from the story and instead he created a fantastic tale. "I knew I had to get him out of there, but he wouldn't move. So I called him names to make him mad. 'Fat tail,' I said. 'Cheese brain! Mousie! Cat meat!' That worked. He lost his temper and ran after me. Before we had reached the corner of the street—boom!"

The young Railway rats were impressed. Roger didn't know I was listening, nor did I bother to correct him.

I was tending our ratlets, who were restless and wanting to play, and I was also turning a question over in my mind. Why did my beautiful Retsina know so much about the Railway rat colony under the train station? She was right about it being safe, but it was not a quiet place. Trains coming and going caused much noise and vibration, as did the feet of humming beans over our heads.

About mid-sunrise a brown and white rat came through the pipe with a string between his teeth. He jumped down, pulled on the string and a black bag plopped down after him. It contained food for the young rats—small segments of pizza. Even at a distance, I could smell tomato and cheese.

Retsina walked slowly over to him. "Hello, Signal."

He was distributing the pizza, but when he heard her voice, he dropped the bag. "You!" he said.

"Yes, me," she replied, smiling.

I must say I found it all somewhat confusing. Clearly Retsina and this brown and white rat knew each other, but she had never mentioned him to me. She brought him over to meet me and our ratlets. "This is my friend, Signal," she said.

Friend? I looked at his dark eyes, one circled with white fur, the other with brown, and my whiskers twitched. He was much too handsome to be a friend. He was also an educated rat. He knew everything about a night train that would begin our journey to Ratenburg. "It goes north-east. You will stay on the train until the final stop tomorrow morning. After that you will need to travel on paw. But be very careful. The way to the mountains is treacherous."

"We're not afraid," said Alpha with great confidence.

Signal looked at her. "You're like your mother," he said. "You have her courage."

Delta had worked out the mathematics of time and train speed. "Going by rail will save us five days of walking, but where do we go after that? There are no maps to Ratenburg."

"That is correct." Signal nodded. "Ratenburg is in a valley between two mountains, and we don't know its exact location. But we do have a map that will take you to the first mountain range. After that, you follow a track." He looked over his shoulder. "Shunter?" he called.

The grey-whiskered rat came forward.

"Bring our map," said Signal.

Shunter disappeared for a moment, then returned with a roll of paper in his mouth. When he put it down and pawed it flat, I saw that it was a label peeled off a tin of baked beans. Beneath faded letters was an equally faded picture of orange beans with a slice of meat resembling bacon. If this was a map, then it was in some kind of code.

"Turn it over," Signal said.

Shunter flicked the paper over and my heart leapt, for indeed this was a detailed map drawn in charcoal on the back of an ordinary label. It showed a line from the end of the railway tracks to the foothills of the mountain range. Somewhere beyond that we would find the valley where a new life lay in the city of Ratenburg. We crowded around the map and Delta wanted to know what the scale was.

"I don't know," Signal replied. "I've never travelled this road. The way has been memorised by Railway rats from one generation to another. My grandfather knew his letters and was able to put his memory on this paper. I can't give you the map. You will have to put every detail into your memories, if you want to know the way."

Retsina placed her paw over mine and I saw that her eyes were shining. "We can do this, Spinnaker."

Now I knew why she had brought us to the den of the Railway rats. She'd known this map existed!

Signal said, "I remind you that I can't let you take this map with you. We don't allow it out of sight. I suggest you try to remember not only the geographical details, but the risks involved. Remember that you're in human land until you get to the mountains, but humans are not the only enemy. Every place has its dangers. The train tracks finish at a town called Sunsweep, situated on the shore of a long, narrow lake of the same name. It would be easy enough for a rat to swim across the lake, if it weren't for the giant eels.

No rat in that water ever gets to the other side. You'll need to find some safe way of crossing the lake."

He then pointed to the other charcoal marks on the back of the baked beans label. Some details were smudged, but he had them in his mind. I knew I also had to remember every word. I told our ratlets to be sure to listen to Uncle Signal. They nodded their little heads and squirmed closer to the map. My beautiful Retsina had her ears and eyes alert, but I wondered why she needed to be so close to that brown and white rat. Did she have difficulty hearing?

There was much distraction. The ground shook and another train roared into the station. The clatter of feet sounded like the rain on the tin roof of an attic I once lived in, but when the noise passed, Signal resumed his instruction. "On the other side of the lake is a farming area known as Sweet Clover Meadows. Corn and barley are grown here, but don't be fooled by a land of plenty. No rats live in the area. Why? Because the humans are hunters and have many dogs that run free during the day to protect the town. That means you can only travel through this area at night."

Signal moved his paw. Further on was Bottomless Bog, a dangerous swamp. After that came the Forest of Perilous Pines, a woodland concealing a deadly threat. This was the nesting place of blue-tailed song hawks that ate small animals. "Here too," said Signal, "you must travel at night when they are asleep." His paw moved again. Grissenden was a humming-bean village where traps and poison were laid for rats passing through. "Don't eat any food you see in that place." Then, near the foot of the mountains was a swing bridge over a deep ravine with a fierce flowing river at the bottom. Signal explained: "The bridge has wooden planks on ropes, arranged as steps for human feet. The gaps between the steps are a danger for rats. If you leap across and slip, you will fall to your death in the river."

Delta leaned over the map. "How do you know all this?"

"It's ancestral knowledge."

"Yes, but how did *they* know?" Delta asked.

"Ah!" Signal flicked his tail as though to begin an important story. "A thousand full moons ago, there was a rat who was half Stable clan—he lived with horses—and half Water rat. He got as far as the swing bridge where he slipped and fell into the river. Having Water rat instincts, he was a remarkable swimmer. The river carried him in a great long curve, right back to Sunsweep Lake. It was this rat who handed down the memory. Now you know why the map stops at the swing bridge. We have no information for the mountains."

With the map still in front of us, I lined up the ratlets in alphabetical order: my adventurous Alpha, dear little Beta, athletic Gamma and thoughtful Delta. "I want you to remember every detail of one place. Alpha, you take Sunsweep Lake. Beta, you memorise Sweet Clover Meadows. Gamma, yours is Bottomless Bog, and Delta, the Forest of Perilous Pines. Retsina, my dear, you are my back-up for the village of Grissenden. As for me, I hope to remember everything, especially the swing bridge."

"What about Uncle Roger?" asked Beta, looking towards our companion, who was talking to the Railway rats and showing no interest at all in the map.

I patted Beta. "Never mind jolly old Uncle Roger. I think he wants to stay here."

Delta murmured, "If you ask me, we'd all like him to stay here."

"Nobody's asking you, Delta," said Alpha. "Remember that Uncle Roger saved Papa's life."

I could but sigh, for what she said was true.

My desire to be rid of the pesky Roger was thwarted, for after the map had been rolled and taken away, and after several trains had come and gone, he grew tired of talking and came back to the nest in the corner for a nap. "Must get ready for the great journey," he said, choosing the softest part of the nest, and folding his front paws over his stomach. He looked so content that I wanted to prod his fat belly, but fathers must set a good example for their children, so I told the ratlets to hush because Uncle Roger was sleeping.

Late that night, Signal provided us with a meal, more pizza, and then guided us back through the drain pipe. We came up between bars in the grating and waited on the unlit end of the platform, where the last part of the train, the luggage wagon, would stop. "Be careful," Signal warned. "When the doors open, go to the back of the wagon where the stores are stacked. You don't want a suitcase thrown on top of you."

The train came roaring out of the blackness and we all shrank away from its bright light. Our youngsters had never seen a train so close before. It was as though a tall building had fallen over onto wheels and was rushing to crush us. Even brave Alpha squeaked and jumped behind her mother. As the great engine passed us, it made a windstorm that parted our fur and set our whiskers flat on our faces. Then it was beyond us, and slowing, and we could see humming-bean faces in the windows. It stopped and doors swung open. In front of us was the last carriage. It was the wagon for luggage, and without windows, but it, too, had an open door with steps.

"Now!" said Signal. "Before the porter gets here with the luggage cart."

I glanced along the station. There were humming beans everywhere. Coming through them was a cart stacked with bags.

"Thank you, Signal," I said, and quickly helped the ratlets up the steps into the wagon. Roger scrambled after them. When I turned to assist Retsina, I saw that she was licking Signal's cheek. "Hurry!" I called. "The train will go without you!"

When we were all inside the luggage wagon, we found a comfortable space between some cardboard cartons. From there, I could see the open door. A humming bean jumped inside and took suitcases from another on the platform. We were safe in the back. I turned to Retsina

and whispered, "I didn't know you were acquainted with the Railway rats."

"Didn't you?" she said, grooming Beta's wind-muddled fur.

"No. You forgot to tell me you had a friend called Signal."

"I didn't forget," she said. "It wasn't important until we were homeless and I started thinking about Ratenburg."

My whiskers twitched. "He seemed a very close friend."

"Yes, he was."

"And very handsome."

Retsina laughed. "Oh Spinnaker! That was long ago, before I met you. You are handsome too, and much nicer! Turn around while I comb your fur. Your back is messy."

When she ran her claws down my back, my sensitive whiskers stopped twitching. "Dearest wife, you were wise to think of Ratenburg. I'm sure it was our family star that guided you to the railway station."

There was a grunt in the darkness and Roger complained, "Will you two stop talking? I need some sleep."

As if in answer, the wagon door slammed shut and a few seconds later the train pulled out of the station.

We were on our way.

CHAPTER THREE

AN UNCOMFORTABLE
NIGHT OF SURPRISES

Dear friend, I wish I could inform you that we slept through that long train journey and woke refreshed, but that was not the case. Signal meant well, but he forgot to tell us that the train stopped at all stations. As soon as we settled down, we experienced unsettling jerks and clangs. The wheels slowed, screeching on the rails, and the wagon shuddered to a stop. Our door opened, some bags were taken out and other bags were brought inside. The humming bean who arranged the luggage wore heavy boots that rang unpleasantly on the metal floor.

We were accustomed to the sounds of metal pipes in the old apartment building but this was much louder. Roger was the only one who slept through the station stops.

My whiskers twitched for the safety of my family. By chewing on the corner of one of the cartons, I discovered they contained cakes of rose soap, nothing edible, and each was heavy enough to stay in place during the bumps and jerks. But supposing these cartons needed to be unloaded at one of the stations? I fossicked about in the dark for an emergency hiding place and found it behind a large canvas bag of mail. If the worst happened, the guards might not see seven rats scuttling for cover. After all, the light was poor.

The worst, however, was not what I expected but something much more hazardous. This, dear friend, is what happened. Although I thought I would not sleep, I must have dozed, for I woke to cries from Retsina. "Alpha got off the train!"

"What?" I saw it was no longer night. Sunlight streamed through the open door, and the guard was lifting out two heavy leather bags. I looked at the ratlets. There were only three. "When?"

Retsina was crying. "Just now! Alpha was among the bags when the train stopped. The guard saw her. She ran out the door. Spinnaker, find her! Quickly!"

"Stay hidden!" I said, and then I raced past the guard

and out the door, falling quite heavily onto the platform. I'm sure the guard didn't see me, but the humming beans who were boarding the train did. They pointed their fingers and made loud noises. I ran alongside the carriages in a large station that had a glass roof. Morning sunshine flooded through, splashing heads and coat-skins and striking the rows of train windows. To one side was another platform with a green train pointed the opposite way. It would be easy to become confused and get back on the wrong train. Where had Alpha gone?

It is not easy to find a small rat among dozens of moving humming-bean feet. In fact, it was impossible. I ran the full length of the station, weaving between shoes, my whiskers twitching like grass in a gale. Why had she left the train? What direction had she taken? At any moment the train doors would close and I would lose the rest of my family. Oh, I assure you, I felt sick with fear. Then I saw her. She was leaping up the step of the carriage next to the engine. Yes, indeed, it was Alpha, my foolish, adventurous daughter. I ran after her, and horror, the whistle sounded and the doors began to close! All I could do was jump into the nearest carriage, several behind the one she had entered. I whisked my tail inside just in time. The door clamped shut behind me.

My vision was blocked by the large legs, but I was aware that something was happening in the carriage. It was only when the owner of the legs dropped a rectangular card on the floor that I realised the guards were looking at passengers' tickets. It was time to move. I slid under the next seat before the owner's eyes and hand made contact.

It occurred to me that the best way to get to Alpha's carriage was under seats and past feet. Few creatures look down while they are talking to each other or staring out of windows. I moved stealthily down the row.

It had not occurred to me that Alpha would be trying to find her way back to the rear of the train. I suppose I should have guessed that my enterprising daughter would be returning to her family. From seat to seat I went, carefully choosing those moments when I was exposed, and about a third of the way along, I picked up her scent. I stopped, sniffed again. Yes, Alpha without doubt! Every good rat parent knows the scent of his or her offspring. But where was she?

Guided by my nose, I found the place where the smell was strongest, and I peered out between two trouser-skins. Here, there were seats facing each other, one occupied by a grown male and a young one, the other by a grown female and a sleeping infant. Next to the infant were some animal toys, and the smallest one was a grey rat. My Alpha was pretending to be a fluffy plaything. Oh, the clever ratlet! She had her eyes closed and was very still, but I could see from the prick of her ears that she was alert. I made a small squeak at a pitch above humming-bean hearing. Alpha's eyes opened. She saw me and blinked in recognition, but did not lose her composure. Slowly, carefully, she slid away from a patchwork dog and crept under the end of the blanket covering the baby.

From there, she dropped over the edge of the seat and ran behind the trouser legs. No one saw her. The big male was reading a newspaper and the female was talking to the young male. Clearly, they were a family.

"Papa!" Alpha whispered in my ear as she snuggled against me. "You were looking for me!"

I whispered back, "Why did you get off the train?"

"I had to, Papa. The guard with the luggage saw me. If I had come back, he would have followed me and found you all. The only thing to do was to jump out and get back in another carriage. Oh Papa, let's go back to the luggage wagon."

"We can't. There's no door between the carriages and the luggage." Then I told her of a plan I had evolved. It had some risk, but could work. We would make our way to the last carriage in the train and wait under the seat nearest the door. When the train stopped at the next station, we would get out of the carriage quickly, before the porter came with the luggage cart, and then scurry into the back wagon.

She flicked her tail. "Good idea, Papa. Let's go."

We worked our way back under the seats, pausing at the end until someone opened the doors between carriages. The train was travelling fast, rocking from side to side, and people going through to the little poo and pee rooms were so busy finding balance that they did not notice two rats behind them. Going almost the full length of the train took a long time and I was concerned that we would stop at a station before we arrived at the last carriage.

As planned, we waited under the last seat in the final carriage. We leapt down the steps and onto the platform of a new station. Someone saw us. There was the old ratophobic cry, "Rats! Vermin!" But we didn't hesitate. Alpha ran ahead of me to the steps of the luggage wagon. The door was wide open, and the humming bean with boots had not yet arrived. I followed and moments later we were behind the soap boxes, reunited with family.

Ah, what a joyful occasion! Retsina had greatly feared that she'd lost both husband and child, and she sobbed against me, soaking my fur. I hugged her. "Beloved wife, you should know I could never leave you," I said, trying to comfort her.

Jolly old Roger lifted his head. "I told her you'd be all right."

Retsina turned and hissed, "You said Spinnaker was gone for good."

Roger put up a paw. "I was merely considering all options," he said calmly.

With the delight of being together again, I had not noticed that all the suitcases had been taken off, and none put in. The train had been at the station for an unusually long time. Big feet clanged across the metal floor and two cartons of soap were lifted. My whiskers twitched. All the contents of the wagon were being unloaded!

"Where are we?" I asked.

Retsina sat up on her hind legs and peered around the edge of the cartons. "I don't know. I think all the humming beans may have got off."

It was Gamma who scrambled up a sheer wall of cardboard to see over the stack of boxes. "I see water," he said. "In the distance! Blue water!"

I looked at Retsina. "Do you think we're at Sunsweep?"

Before she could answer, the guard came back and lifted two more cartons. Now there was no doubt in my mind. We had to get off. I said to the ratlets, "This is as far as the train goes. The next time the guard comes in, we wait until he goes out, carrying the boxes, and we follow him. As he steps down to the platform, we come down behind him and run away from the train. Retsina, Roger, you lead the way. I will go last, should we be discovered and pursued."

"And if they catch you?" Retsina was worried.

I smiled. "My dear, I don't fancy the taste of humming bean, but if necessary, I will bite."

I was so confident that the guard would be too busy to see us that I failed to notice the twitch of my whiskers. The heavy-footed humming bean grabbed another two cartons and turned towards the door. We slid out of hiding, Retsina first, Roger behind her, the four ratlets, and me at the back. The big boots went down the steps to a half-filled cart that stood on the platform. A line of grey fur slid down after him and turned sharply left. I followed, but the guard saw me. One of those heavy boots came down on my tail and I was caught! My claws scrabbled uselessly on the concrete as I watched the gap between me and my family widen.

The guard roared something and bent over. I struggled

but his boot was crushing my tail and the pain was most unpleasant. I could do nothing to save myself.

I saw his hand come down. He was reaching for my head. The shadow of that broad palm and wide fingers came over me with the promise of death, and I struggled again. Then I sank my teeth into his thumb and held on.

He howled and tried to shake me off his hand. But his boot was still on my tail and every movement sent great pain through me. At last, he lifted his foot, gave a final shake of his fist and I fell back on the concrete. His boot rose up to crush me, but I was away like the wind, dragging my poor injured tail behind me.

Retsina and the others were waiting in the tall weeds at the end of the platform. I didn't want to alarm my family, so I tried to make light of the incident, saying that the guard's thumb tasted like mouldy cheese—although, to tell the truth, my tail was so sore that all I wanted to do was go away by myself and howl like a baby ratlet.

My fine tail was broken, dear friend. I knew it. I would have a lump near the end of my caudal appendage, and forever I would be known as Spinnaker the Ship rat with the crooked tail.

CHAPTER FOUR

OUR ATTEMPT TO CROSS
SUNSWEEP LAKE

Gamma said he knew the direction of the lake. He had seen flat blue water through the door of the luggage wagon. He led us through the high weeds, jumping every now and then to check his bearings. He made sure that we walked around the outskirts of the town and not through it.

Because I had convinced my wife that my experience with the train guard's boot was trivial, she concerned herself with keeping the family together. If the truth be known, I could have used a little sympathy for my poor tail. It dragged behind, reminding me of my injury every time it encountered a small obstacle such as a dandelion bush or a dried twig. Roger walked beside me, full of cheerful talk.

"That's the worst part of the journey over, Spinny, me lad."

I did not respond to his prattle, and I wished he would move away. I lifted my tail over the roots of willow trees, and in a mood of blackness, I hoped that the luggage guard would get a thousand flea bites on the most tender parts of his body.

Roger went on: "After that train ride, a trip across the lake will be a piece of cheese."

Alpha turned. "You're forgetting about the giant eels, Uncle Roger."

Jolly Roger snorted. "Pirate rats eat eels for breakfast."

My tail may have been sore, but my nose was in excellent working order, and I sniffed the weeds and long grass for any sign of hidden cat. In several places I noted old dog pee and some mouse droppings, but there was no cat odour, and no nasty surprises. Past the willow trees, the earth smell suggested dampness, and I knew we were somewhere near the shore of the lake.

It was Alpha who had been given the memory task for Sunsweep Lake, and she, too, was sniffing the earth. "Don't go near the water," she said to her brothers and sister. She glanced back at Roger. "These eels eat rats for breakfast."

We came to a clearing that was some kind of humming-bean camp on the shore of the lake. Through the last grass stalks we saw two houses on wheels and a small fabric house pinned to the earth with poles and ropes. There were no humming beans to be seen, but some of their coloured skins were hanging on a line between the two houses on wheels. The lake was as Delta had described it, calm and bright blue, with a shore on the other side at a distance of one city street—not far at all. If the water was full of rat-eating giant eels, they were well hidden below the smooth surface.

Alpha stepped out into the clearing and at once there was the shrill loudness of a barking dog. She jumped back into the grass. This was the worst kind of dog: a terrier that specialised in the extermination of rats and rabbits. But the noise stayed at the same distance, and when I put out my head to investigate, I saw a sharp-faced terrier jumping

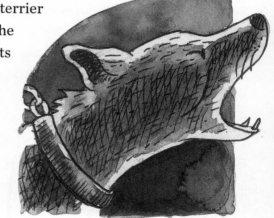

up and down on a rope fastened to a wooden kennel. The animal was tied and couldn't reach us. We were in no danger.

We all came out to the shore of damp earth and grass that had been given a haircut. From our shadows, I estimated middle day. The sun overhead gleamed on the water and the air was still. Further along our side of the lake was a small colony of houses on wheels and a wooden jetty that looked as though a road had waded into the water and stopped, perhaps afraid of the eels. I suggested this to Alpha but she merely said, "Oh Papa, you've become very fanciful in your old age." I realised then that my ratlets were growing up and could no longer relate to my funny baby rat stories. That fact, together with the pain in my tail and the barking dog, made me rather sad.

I was in a melancholy daydream and didn't notice that Beta had gone to the water's edge. She was thirsty, and as she bent to put her nose into the water, Alpha and Retsina shrieked. On the water in front of Beta there appeared a V-shaped ripple. She didn't see it, but I did. I sprang forward, a great leap, grabbed Beta's tail between my teeth and yanked her away from the lake's edge. As I did so, a head broke the surface. I swear to you, my friend, that head was bigger than the head of a mature humming bean. It was shining greenish-black with pale, round eyes, a wide-open mouth and sharp teeth that sloped back into its mouth. The mouth snapped shut where Beta's head had been. There was a great splashing in the shallows as a dark body as long and thick as a tree trunk turned in a semicircle. The tail scraped the bottom, stirring up mud, then the giant eel headed back to the depths.

Beta was shaking all over and squeaking with every breath. Poor little ratlet! No doubt, I was not the only one who now had a sore tail, but I had snatched her from certain death.

Retsina and Delta comforted Beta. Alpha said, "I told you not to go near the water!" Her voice was severe because she was also in shock. It had all been so sudden.

Delta informed us, "We shouldn't be surprised that it almost came ashore. In wet weather, eels can travel over land from—"

"Stop! Stop!" Roger put his front paws over his ears. His mouth was drawn back from his teeth and his eyes were closed. "That's enough! There's no way you'll get me over that lake. If you want to be eel bait, that's your business. I'm setting sail for Sunsweep town and a cosy nest at the back of a tavern. Bye, shipmates! It's been nice knowing you."

He wasn't bluffing. He was leaving us. He ran towards the long grass and, without so much as a word or wave of his tail, he disappeared. I was surprised, but without regret. The journey to Ratenburg would be much easier without Roger.

Delta looked thoughtful. "He had a point, Papa. How do we get across that lake? Are we capable of building an eel-proof boat?"

We were quiet for a while, all except Beta, who was still making an occasional sobbing hiccup, and the crazy dog that leapt on the end of its rope. "I'll get you!" it was barking. "I'll bite your heads off and spit out your brains!"

I ignored it. In my opinion, even pedigree terriers are ill bred. My concern was the giant eels. In good conditions, rats are capable swimmers, but none of us would last ten seconds in that water. A boat was needed. But what boat?

Alpha sat beside me. "Papa, the lake is my responsibility. Remember? I'm going over there." She pointed her nose at the camping place. "I'll find a boat for us."

"Sweetheart, what would six rats do with a humming-bean boat?"

"I didn't mean that kind of boat," she said. "Something that will float. You know, like a big balloon."

"Eels have sharp teeth," I reminded her.

She patted me on the back. "I know that, Papa. I'll return soon."

I called after her, "Don't go near the dog!"

Retsina and I watched Alpha run through the shadows to the houses on wheels. We knew that our daughter had much good sense, but she was also the one who took risks and we didn't like the way the terrier's barking changed to a coaxing growl. The dog was daring her to come closer.

After a while, Beta recovered from her frightening experience. I saw the marks made by my teeth on her tail, but at least her tail was still straight and not broken like mine. She did not mention the hurt. "Thank you, Papa," she said.

Retsina also sat next to me. "Spinnaker, I'm anxious. Do you think Roger had the right idea? Consider our ratlets! Surely a nest in the town is safer than attempting to cross that water."

"Darling wife, it's you who has always had the dream of living in Ratenburg."

She nodded. "I know. I've heard about it ever since I was a tiny ratlet, but I never imagined it would be so difficult to go there."

"What if it wasn't difficult? Think about that! If the way to Ratenburg was easy, that perfect city would be overrun with rats. Everyone would go there! Because the way is difficult, only the strong and intelligent—like us—can survive the journey."

My dear wife still looked worried. "I hope you're right."

"I know I'm right. Look, my dear, look at my whiskers! Are they twitching? No! That means we'll get safely across the lake."

"It might mean that we'll find a safe nest in the town," she said, and I realised she was deeply disturbed. This morning she believed she had lost me and Alpha at a foreign railway station. Then her gentle Beta had been almost eaten by a giant eel. It was all too much for a motherly rat who'd been born at the back of a first-class Greek restaurant. I licked behind her left ear. "Don't worry, my love. Think of our family star. We'll be safely guided."

When Alpha came back, she seemed very excited. "I've found a boat!"

"What kind of boat?" Retsina asked.

"Where?" I said.

Alpha answered both questions. "It's a humming-bean cooking pot. Come! I'll show you!"

Retsina stayed with the other three while I followed Alpha to the space between the two houses with wheels. Under the cloth-skin line was a fireplace, and nearby on a shelf was a large pot and cooking tools. Alpha pointed to the pot. "No eel will bite that!"

I considered it: a strong metal pot with a handle on each side. Certainly it would contain a family of six.

But there was a problem. "How will we propel it across the lake?"

"With oars!" said Alpha, indicating two cooking tools: a wooden spoon and a long-handled food scraper. She stood on her hind paws to touch a handle on the pot. "The oars can fit through these loops."

I was pleased that she had done so well. "My clever ratlet!" I cried.

When we told Retsina, she was still anxious. "How will we get it to the water?"

"That's what family is for," Alpha replied.

It did take all of us to push the pot down the slope to the water's edge, and the closer we got, the more cautious we became. Poor Beta was terrified. But no eel came into the shallows to investigate. I suspect that a metal saucepan was less attractive than a plump little rat.

All the while, the terrible terrier was barking its anger with a madness that had it straining at the end of the rope. We took no notice but kept well out of its reach when we went back for the tools that would be our oars. I dragged one and Retsina dragged the other. Now we had a boat sitting on the edge of the water, two oars in place, but how would we launch it? I suggested we get the ratlets on board first. That was a simple matter. Each climbed up my back and over the top of the pot. Their weight inside it, however, anchored it firmly in the mud.

I looked beyond it, checking the surface of the lake for threatening ripples. All was calm. The only threats came from the dog dancing at the end of its tether and telling us what it would do with us.

"Push!" I said to Retsina.

We both pushed as hard as we could. The pot moved a little but was still aground.

"Another push!" I said. "One, two, three!" The pot moved a paw space so that it was half in the water.

"Try again!" said Retsina.

We were both so occupied with launching our pot boat that we hadn't noticed that the dog had stopped barking. It was Alpha who told us why. "Papa! Mama! Hurry! The dog is biting through its rope."

I glanced back. It was true. The terrier was chewing the tether that kept us safe. "Push!" I yelled at Retsina.

How we strained against the pot! It was stubbornly slow but each push was a little easier, as the water took some of the pot's weight.

"Hurry, Papa!" Alpha screamed.

One more heave and the pot bobbed a little. I knew that when Retsina and I got on board, it would go aground again. We needed to take it out further, but that risked us becoming eel bait.

"The dog's loose! It's coming!"

We waded deeper, steering the pot out, then I helped

Retsina up the side. She tumbled over and reached for my paw. Meanwhile, Alpha and Gamma had taken an oar each. Barking furiously, the dog raced down the beach, but by the time it got to the water's edge, our pot was bobbing nicely and moving with strokes of the cooking tools. Retsina and I took control of the oars because we were stronger and taller on our hind legs. We were now too deep for wading, and the angry dog was yelling insults from the rim of water. "I'll get you! I'll bite out your eyes! I'll bite off your tails!"

I laughed. "Do your worst, you stupid mongrel!"

I should not have taunted it. In the heat of the moment, I had forgotten that dogs are good swimmers. The terrier made a determined leap into the water and came after us with strong, sure strokes. Its paws were much faster than our makeshift oars.

"Go back!" I yelled at it. "Come any closer and I'll hit you with this paddle!"

My threat was feeble and the dog knew it. Although it was not a big dog, it was certainly bigger than a family of rats. It would tip the pot over and we'd all find ourselves in the stomachs of hungry eels.

Now the terrier was almost upon us. Its paws paddled fast and it grinned up at me, certain of victory. I looked at the sharp teeth embedded in that smile. Then I observed a disturbance in the water behind the dog's short tail.

The dog's expression suddenly changed. It turned its head, but before it could yelp, it went under the water and disappeared.

Our pot rocked slightly in small waves and then became steady again, as though nothing had happened. Only Beta cried for the dog. I may have mentioned that Beta is very tender-hearted. The rest of us were too relieved to feel any sympathy for a terrier taken by a giant eel. I glanced over Retsina's shoulder and saw we were nearly at the opposite shore. It was indeed a narrow lake.

"You were right," Retsina said to me.

"Right?" I looked at her. "About what?"

"Everything!" She smiled. "We were safe. Your whiskers didn't twitch once."

CHAPTER FIVE

NOT ALL CLOVER MEADOWS ARE SWEET

Having successfully crossed the lake, we left our pot boat and oars in a patch of rushes. We were confident now that we could get to Ratenburg, but if we wanted to return home, then the boat with two oars could be useful again.

Retsina and I helped our ratlets through the rushes and up a low hill. The view from the top was very fine indeed: a country road with humming-bean houses, barns for cows and hay, and large fields of grass, barley and corn. It was surely a land of plenty and would be ideal for rats, were it not so populated with dogs. We could hear hounds barking to each other from farm to farm.

Beta, who had the memory for this part of the journey, reminded us, "The farmers have trained their dogs to get rid of rabbits and rats. Uncle Signal said we must travel at night."

I was still a little sensitive about that brown and white Railway rat. I glanced at Retsina, then said to Beta, "Uncle Signal has never travelled the map. Nor is that likely. Rats like him have usually descended from humming-bean pets. Their ancestors lived in cages with mousie toys."

"Nonsense!" snapped Retsina. "Signal comes from a long line of very intelligent Laboratory rats. His grand-mother trained humming beans to give her a piece of cheese when she ran through a maze. How many rats can do that?"

I sniffed. "I was merely making the observation that he has never been here." I drew my tail around me, aware that it was still very sore. "I don't care what kind of ancestry he has. I'm saying that a map isn't the journey. Did the great Signal tell us that the train would stop at every station? Did he warn us about the terrible terrier?"

"I don't have to listen to this!" said Retsina.

Delta came between us. "Will you two stop shouting? We've had enough dog attention for the day."

Beta said, "Papa, Mama, I've been thinking. We need a safe place to rest until dark. If the rabbits have been hunted, there should be some empty rabbit tunnels in the fields."

Retsina and I were surprised that our gentle Beta should have such a clever idea. We also felt somewhat embarrassed that we had quarrelled in front of the ratlets. I congratulated Beta, and Retsina suggested that when we came upon a suitable rabbit tunnel, we should find a ripe corncob to take down it. With much enthusiasm and some caution, we set off down the hill. We could hear the dogs but didn't see them, and since their barking was conversational, we assumed that they didn't know we were in their territory.

The first to locate an empty rabbit burrow was Gamma. We thought this was a lucky find until we discovered vacant holes all over the hillside. Some still smelled faintly of rabbit, while others had been long empty and had grass roots growing through their ceilings. I felt a chill. I was not particularly fond of rabbits but they were harmless creatures and I did not wish them ill. That there should be so many forsaken tunnels suggested either a great migration or a great slaughter. I suspected the latter and was convinced it would not be good for us to linger in Sweet Clover Meadows. We would rest until dark and then recommence our journey.

The chosen tunnel was near the corn field. Gamma ran up a stalk and severed a plump, ripe cob. It fell with a heavy plop and we rolled it into the tunnel opening. Ah, what pleasure! There can surely be no greater delicacy than kernels of corn fresh from the plant. After the feast, we lay at the bottom of the burrow, utterly content, and Delta said, "Papa, tell us the story of brave Grandpa Mizzen."

"You want to hear that again?" I asked.

"Yes, yes!" they all said, and Retsina added, "If you are not too tired."

"Papa Mizzen and Mama Sloop lived on an old cargo ship that went around the world carrying containers as big as houses."

"Tell us what was in them!" cried Beta.

"Bunches of green bananas from Ecuador. Car engines from Italy."

They knew this by heart and chanted with me. "Truffles from France. Sausages from Germany. Herrings from Norway."

"You left out olives from Greece," said Retsina.

"Olives and delicious retsina wine from Greece," I said. "But one day the ship with a cargo of containers hit some rocks and began to sink. So what do rats always do?"

"They always leave a sinking ship!" our ratlets shouted.

"Not my father," I told them. "He stood bravely on the deck while all the other rats dived overboard and swam for the shore. 'The captain goes down with the ship!' he said. Mama Sloop was in the water, waiting for him. 'You are not the captain, you fool!' she said. 'You are my husband! Jump!' But he would not jump. She shouted, 'You are the father of my ratlets.' 'What ratlets?' he said. 'We don't have any babies.' 'We will have some soon,' said Mama Sloop. 'Jump or I'll come up there and push you off.' So my brave papa, Mizzen Rat, jumped into the water and swam to the shore with Mama Sloop. The next day seven ratlets were born on a ledge under a wharf. I was the last to arrive."

Gamma said, "Now tell us how you and Mama met."

"Another time," I told him. "We've had a long day and we're all tired. Go to sleep."

Full of good food, and safe in the darkness of the rabbit burrow, we went into such a deep sleep, we lost a sense of time.

It was an unfamiliar noise that woke me, a scraping sound. Instantly alert, I eased away from the tangle of slumbering fur and crept up the dark tunnel. The scratching noise grew louder. Large paws raked at the opening, and then a snout plugged the hole. Yes, it was a dog, one much larger than the terrier, a hound of some sort with a great bulge of sniffing nose. It could smell me. I was sure of that. Although there was almost no light, I could see the nostrils dilating. The beast pushed harder and its muzzle came into the hole, floppy jowls and a wet mouth, breath stinking of rotten meat. But the hole was too tight to allow the mouth to open, so I knew that I could safely attack. I lunged at the nose and clamped my teeth onto it.

The hound pulled back so quickly that I was yanked out of the burrow. Fortunately, the dog was too surprised by the attack to take advantage of the fact that a rat was dangling in front of its face. It shook its head, I fell off and in an instant I was back down the hole. But in that instant I registered two things: it was already night and the hound was loose. So much for Signal's information about dogs being tied up when it was dark!

The hound went loping off, whimpering, but I knew it would be back. There were stories about rat-hunters, how a dog would stand guard until a humming bean came with fire and smoke to drive rats into the open. I went back down the burrow and woke the family. It was time to move.

I didn't tell my wife about the hound. I didn't need to. She sniffed as we came out of the burrow, and whispered, "Dog."

I said in her ear, "Gone."

There was no way of knowing how many dogs were roaming about in the dark, so I chose a path through the corn field. If a dog did pick up our scent, it would not be able to find us without making a noise. Corn plants rustle and rattle, and these were planted close, only a rat's distance apart. We ran in our usual formation, Retsina in front, the ratlets and then me, pausing a couple of times to listen for dogs. There was distant barking but nothing close. I looked up past corn leaves, and in a small patch of dark sky, I saw a magnificent omen. "Look, everyone! Our family star!"

Six noses pointed skyward. Six sets of whiskers moved at the edges of smiles. There was our beautiful star shining down on us. Rats backward!

Then an all too familiar voice said, "It's a planet!"

I jumped, certain that this was in my imagination, but no, from around a corn stalk came Pirate rat Roger. "I thought it was you," he said.

My mind was in such a state of confusion, I could not utter a word.

He patted his stomach, even rounder than usual. "I'm sick of corn. I've been here all day."

Retsina said, "How did you get across the lake?"

"Not a problem," he said. "Sunsweep town didn't have a cosy tavern, so I decided to cross the lake. The humans have a ferry boat that goes back and forth. Did you see the jetty? I hid in a picnic basket and had a free lunch with my ride. How did you get across?"

Our ratlets wanted to tell him but I hushed them. "The dogs will hear us! Walk quietly!"

Jolly old Roger fell into line in front of me. He glanced upwards and smiled. "It's the planet Venus," he said.

"Don't be such a mouse!" I snapped.

We walked most of the night, over fields and then on the edge of the road, because Beta was sure that humming beans would not allow dogs where there was traffic. A few cars went past. When we heard them coming, we bellied down in the grass and were undetected. Sometimes a distant hound would pick up our scent on the still air and bark an alarm. Since no dog came after us, I thought that perhaps dogs were confined at night, and the one that had tried to dig our burrow was an exception.

The sky in the east turned grey, and we were still in the Sweet Clover Meadows. We would soon have to find a daytime hiding place. If the hounds were let loose during the day, no hole in the ground would be safe.

"We need to hide before they're set free," Beta said, hopping nervously from paw to paw.

We were all in agreement, but an empty rabbit tunnel was not a practical solution.

"What about a hay barn, shipmate?" Roger asked.

I was still ignoring him, but I thought it a good idea.

Perhaps not a hay barn, I decided, but some kind of tool shed where we could safely hide in the rafters.

"Plenty of hay barns," Roger insisted.

I was silent, still angry that he had travelled effortlessly across the lake in a picnic basket when we'd had such a struggle in a metal pot. Some things were simply not fair!

At last I located a suitable shed along a minor road. It was open on one side and contained a row of complex machinery we did not recognise, although Roger was certain that some hanging objects were lights for humans who had poor vision. "Four lights in each section of the shed," he said. "Notice that the lights are movable and can be hung over a clear work space."

"Very interesting," I said, "but this is not finding us suitable shelter."

"Papa! Up here!" Gamma had climbed up a long piece of rough wood that supported the roof. Under the edge of the roof was a recess well out of the reach of rat-hunting dogs. Even if they caught our scent, they would not be able to see us or reach us. If by chance we were discovered by humming beans, there was ample space for escape along the rafters and out to the other side of the building. Once again, I felt great pride in our ratlets, who were proving themselves to be intelligent and resourceful. We joined Gamma on the high ledge of the shed and were settling down when a dog barked.

"That's close," said Retsina. "It's not yet daybreak and the dogs are loose already."

"What's that other noise?" said Alpha.

I listened. "A male humming bean."

"No," Alpha replied. "Not that. The crowd noise."

She was right. A crowd of creatures was approaching the shed with at least one dog and a humming bean. As they came closer, the sound was louder, but for the life of me, I could not see what it was all about. We lay still as the assortment of noise increased—a low bellowing, a shuffling, a snorting, a squishing of feet in mud, with dog barks and sometimes instruction from the humming bean. "Get in behind there!"

"I know what this is," said Retsina.

She was smiling, so I knew we were not in danger. "What?" I asked.

"Those very large creatures are cows, and this is a milking shed."

Being a Ship rat, I had never seen a milking shed, although I vaguely associated the word cow with milk. If someone had asked me where milk came from, I would have remembered a glass or plastic container left out on tables in the apartment building. I put my head over the ledge and looked down as the large furred creatures entered the shed. They certainly were huge—bigger than bicycles and slightly smaller than cars—and their odour was very strong. More came into the space in front of the shed. Alpha joined me and peered down, amazed at the number and size of these animals. She said to Beta, who was behind her, "They have tusks on their head and four black feet and a huge hand with four fingers."

Without looking, Retsina said calmly, "That's not a hand. It's an udder full of milk. And the thing with four tubes is not a light, but a milking machine. It goes on the four teats on the udder and takes out the milk. The milk is then made into delicious cheese and yoghurt."

I stared at her. "How do you know all this?"

She licked her lips. "Feta cheese. Greek yoghurt. Spinnaker dear, you haven't had the benefit of a restaurant education."

I glanced back at Jolly Roger. "You said those tubes were lights."

He shrugged. "I was only joking."

The humming bean came in and switched on the machines, which roared and rattled, drowning the noise of the cows. The big beasts went into the spaces made for them and the tubes were plugged near their back legs. There were slosh-slosh sounds as the smell of milk mixed with cow breath, cow poo and dog smell. I found it all very interesting, and encouraged the ratlets to come to the edge, one at a time, to witness the taking of milk. Not once did the humming bean in the blue cloth-skin

look up at us. He was much too busy washing each cow's udder, putting on the tubes, then removing them and opening a door to release the cow and make room for the next.

Many cows went through. The sun was up and flies were buzzing by the time the last cow went out its door. The farmer then turned on a hose to clean the floor, which was now covered with cow poo, a dark green colour, the consistency of mud after rain. I watched. I had always been amused by the humming bean need for separate poo and pee rooms, but now saw some logic in it. To have creatures excreting in a place where food is produced is a back to front way of doing things.

When the cleaning was done, and the floor and pipes in the shed were dripping with water, the dog stood up and followed the humming bean from the shed. We heard boots crunching gravel on the little road.

I was surprised that the dog did not detect us, but then guessed that the strong cow and milk odours would mask any smell of rat. By now, all the ratlets were asleep against the rafter, and I did not wake them. For the last two days they'd had little rest, and a long sleep was greatly needed. Retsina and Roger agreed, for they, too, were tired. We would stay in the roof of the shed until evening.

Before long, Roger was lying on his back, paws across his chest, snoring at the far end of the ledge. Retsina curled up with the ratlets, her nose close to Beta's neck, her tail around the other three, her eyes closed. They all looked very peaceful.

I, on the other hand, was measuring time since the last meal of corn kernels. The smell of fresh milk brought juices to my mouth. It would do no harm, I decided, to see where the milk was. I turned my ears to outside noises. Certainly, there were dogs barking, but all in the distance. The only close sounds were Roger's snoring and the harmless chatter of sparrows on the roof. I could risk a small expedition of discovery.

I climbed down the rough wooden support to the concrete floor, still wet in patches. On the far side, a white-painted door was ajar, leaving a gap wide enough for a grown rat. I found myself in an enclosed room on two levels. On the lower level was more machinery, but up four concrete steps was the biggest pot I have ever seen. It was of the same shining metal and shape as the boat pot we had used to cross the lake, but a thousand times bigger. A mountainous pot! The sides were so smooth that even our acrobatic Gamma would not have been able to climb it. I was sure, though, that this was where the milk was stored.

I was a Ship rat who had never been on a real ship, but I had inherited all my parents' instincts about engine rooms and pipes. If I looked at a problem long enough,

I would solve it. Could I use a rope to climb up the pot? No. That wouldn't work. Was there something else I could use as a ladder? No. Nothing. I scratched my head. The sweet smell of fresh milk overwhelmed me, and my stomach made hungry sounds. How did the milk get into the pot? Ah, there was the answer! From a machine there was a metal pipe connected to a wrinkled white hose and, if I wasn't mistaken, that hose went into the opening at the top of the pot mountain. Oh yes!

The machine was silent, still and cold. Quickly, I ran up it, up the metal pipe and then the plastic hose, my paws easily skimming over the lumpy, bumpy surface. Now I was on top of the enormous round metal tub and looking over the end of the plastic hose at enough milk to feed all the rats in the world. There was one small problem. This sea of milk was beyond reach. It was at least half a tail's length below the rim of the pot. How frustrating! There was, however, a tiny puddle of milk inside the opening of the plastic hose. I would at least, have a taste. I perched on top of the hose end. Normally, I would have wrapped my tail around it as a precaution but you may remember, dear friend, that my tail was rather tender. I simply balanced myself as best I could, and leaned down, my tongue fully stretched. I could see the drops of milk. I could almost taste them. I moved forward a little and then, suddenly, my mouth, eyes and nose were full of milk.

I had fallen into the pot!

I came up gasping. The milk was cold. I swam to the edge and tried to climb out. My paws slipped on the smooth metal. So I turned and swam back to the pipe but that was also too high. Although I tried leaping, it was to no avail because there was nothing solid to leap from. So I tried the metal sides all around the pot. My claws made scratching sounds but would not grip.

The seriousness of the situation replaced my hunger. I could not get out! I, Spinnaker of the Ship rat clan, would drown in a sea of milk! I paddled back and forth.

"Help!" I cried. "Help! Help! Help!"

My squeaks were pathetically small and I knew they would not be heard. The milk pot was far from my family, who were all asleep. A great sorrow rose up in me. Not only would I drown in this white sea, but my family would never know what had happened to me. Retsina might conclude that I'd been eaten by a dog. My children could believe I'd run away and deserted them. Oh, what a terrible state I was in!

My legs felt weak. I was growing tired and I could not even say farewell. I thought of my darling wife Retsina with her large, soft eyes, and my precious ratlets and I wept bitterly. What would they do without me? "Forgive me!" I cried. "Forgive me!"

"What for?" someone said.

It was Roger. He was sitting on top of the plastic pipe and his mouth was white with milk.

My fortune had changed! "Help me!" I said. "Get me out of this!"

"How?" he asked.

I thought for a moment. "Let your tail down. I'll grab it and climb up."

He shook his head. "You'll pull me into the vat and we'll both be in trouble." He peered down at me. "Tell you what, shipmate. I'll go back to the edge of the vat where I've got something to hang onto. You can hold my tail there."

"Thank you!" I said. "Oh, thank you, Roger!"

He ran back along the pipe to the place where it came over the edge. With his hind legs gripping the pipe and his front paws on the rim of the giant pot, he flicked his tail over the side. Wonderful, a rat rope! My relief was inexpressible. Never again would I have an unkind thought or word about Roger. The tip of his tail went into the milk and there in front of my nose was the way out of my predicament.

I grabbed hold of his tail, but my wet paws couldn't get a grip.

"Hang on!" he yelled.

"Roger, I can't! Your tail is slippery."

"Shiver me timbers! It's you made it slippery. You got milk on it. Try again!"

I tried again and fell back into the milk. I choked and spat. "It's no good. Roger, I'm sorry. I'll have to hold your tail with my mouth."

"Don't you dare!" he cried, and his tail twitched.

Before he could raise it beyond my reach, I grasped it between my teeth.

At this point, dear friend, I have to leave out some of the story. I can't repeat what Roger said about me. The words are not fit for a book, and they made me think that Roger may have had a Pirate background after all. I didn't answer for fear of letting go but hung on, my teeth clenched on his tail, while he struggled to pull me up. Actually, I think he was struggling to get away. The effect was the same. I gradually came out of the milk, up the side of the pot and onto the plastic pipe. The procedure took a long time and we were both exhausted when it was over.

"You've ruined my tail!" he moaned, examining tooth marks.

"I'm sorry, Roger. I'm very sorry." I looked at him. "You are a great hero. Did you hear me calling for help?"

"No."

"So how did you know I was there?"

"I wasn't looking for you," he said. "I wanted some milk and I heard you calling. What on earth made you jump into the vat?"

"I didn't. I fell off the pipe." Then I told him how I had tried to get the drops of milk.

He frowned. "That was a silly way of getting a drink. Why didn't you turn on the tap?"

"What tap?"

"The tap at the bottom of the vat. You lean on it and you get milk. Lean on it again and the milk stops. Come on down and I'll show you."

We walked slowly down the pipes, over the machine and onto the floor. Roger took me to the front of the giant pot and showed me the tap. There was a pool of milk under it. "Help yourself," he said.

I shook my head.

"Well, at least lick yourself clean," he told me.

I couldn't even do that. I would be happy if I didn't taste milk again for the rest of my life. I went back into the shed and rolled in a puddle of water until my fur had lost that sticky whiteness.

Roger made a great fuss about his tail, although it was no more hurt than Beta's. Both would heal in a day or two, whereas the damage inflicted by the train guard to my tail was permanent. I crawled up to our shelter under the roof, and in spite of the trauma I had experienced, I slept. I was extremely tired. But I was awake again well before nightfall, because no one had informed me that cows were milked twice a day. The sun had scarcely begun its descent in the west than those big creatures returned—same dog, same humming bean, same noise and mess. It was well past sunset when the shed was returned to a quiet and clean state and we were all able to come out of hiding.

The ratlets were hungry. Jolly old Roger was pleased to turn the tap on the pot so that they could drink the milk. "It'll be cold," he told them. "The vat has a refrigerator in it."

"Have some, Spinnaker," said Retsina. "It's delicious."

I had not told them about my accident. "No thanks. I'm not hungry."

Roger turned off the tap. "It should be delicious," he said to Retsina. "You husband has been swimming in it." Then he turned his smile to me. "Tell them about your swim, Spinny."

So I told them. If I hadn't, he would have done so.

Retsina looked alarmed, but Roger laughed at her anxiety. "I don't know how many times I'll have to save his life," he said.

"Don't be such a mouse!" I muttered under my breath.

CHAPTER SIX

WE DISCOVER THE BOTTOMLESS BOG

A fine rain accompanied us that night and although it was cold, it brought two favours: it prevented our scent from reaching dogs, and it washed the last traces of milk from my fur. I wanted to forget about that near disaster. There was not much chance of that, however, for Roger kept reminding me of my swim in the milk vat, and the tooth marks I had put in his tail. I was grateful to him for saving my life. Of course I was. But several rounds of thank you were not enough. It was a never-ending supply of gratitude he wanted, and I struggled with my irritation. When I thought of Roger crossing the lake in a picnic basket, Roger turning the tap for milk, anger flared up in me. I walked a little faster to avoid his talk, but he always caught up.

"The milk tanker comes to collect the milk," he said. "Imagine what the driver would have said when he found a drowned rat."

"I know, I know. If it hadn't been for you, Roger, I'd be dead." I tried to shorten his story.

"You might have blocked his intake pipe," he said cheerfully.

We were nearing the outskirts of Sweet Clover Meadows, passing more trees and fewer humming-bean houses. We had chosen to travel at the edge of the road, rather than cross unknown country, for although there was traffic, we were outside the bright focus of the eyes of cars and trucks. I knew we would need to stop before we came to the Bottomless Bog. Although our night-sight was adequate, we would need full daylight to detect the dangers, whatever they were, of the swamp.

Having slept most of the day, Retsina and the ratlets had fine energy. The girls and Gamma wanted to know more about Ratenburg. I told them, "Its beauty is beyond our imagination. The nests are lined with silk and swans-down. The food barns are always full—"

"So Ratenburg has silkworms and swans," said Delta.

"No, only rats," I said.

"Then how do they get—"

"Delta, they may use product from other creatures, but only rats can live there. Every creature has its own natural home. Why do you think humming beans suffer from ratophobia? It's because they've built their cities for humming beans and we have invaded them. Those cities don't belong to rats. Birds have their nests in trees. Tigers have jungles in Africa. Rats have Ratenburg."

"India," said Delta.

"What?"

"Tigers live in India. There are no tigers in Africa."

"Are you sure?"

"I am sure, Papa."

"Well then, tigers in India. It makes no difference to the point I'm trying to make. All rats want to go to Ratenburg because it belongs to rats."

"Not all," said Delta. "Personally, I believe the basement of another humming-bean apartment building would suit us just as well."

"And face more ratophobia?" I tried to see his face in the dark. "My boy, I'm tired of moving from place to place. I'm tired of fighting wars. I want to live in a place where rats can truly feel at home."

He was silent after that, and I was likewise, remembering places where I had lived for a time. Let me tell you, dear friend, all my places of abode have been of short or very short occupancy. I have only infant memories of the wharf where I was born. Dogs and poisonous smoke guns were brought in to exterminate rats. My father fled with me and my brother, Hawser, and we went inland, taking refuge in the attic of a humming-bean house that had a fine vegetable garden. I remember eating strawberries and green peas and wondering where my mother, sisters and other brothers were. We were not at the garden house for long. The owners bought a cat. So we moved on and that became the pattern of our lives, each move made to avoid a danger.

Papa Mizzen said he would take me away on a ship, but before that happened, he and Hawser disappeared. I didn't know what happened to them, but I desperately wanted to believe they had gone to Ratenburg. Then one day I met Retsina, the beautiful rat who lived in a drain behind the Greek restaurant. She had always lived there, but the drain was overcrowded, so together we made a nest in the old apartment building I described at the beginning of this book. We had our four ratlets and I believed I had at last found permanence. How wrong I was! How utterly wrong! As this thought overwhelmed me, I gave a sigh that must have come from the depths of my heart, because Retsina hurried to my side.

"Spinnaker dear, what's wrong?"

Her sympathy brought moisture to my eyes. "Dearest wife, I have a confession to make. I have failed you and our ratlets. I have not been a good provider. Here we are, wandering in the dark, no food, no home, no idea of where we are going or what we will find when we get there. We're vagabonds."

"Not vagabonds, Spinnaker. We're pilgrims on our way to Ratenburg."

Her words failed to cheer me. "I have put your lives at risk," I said. "What dedicated father does that to his family? Look at me, Retsina! I'm a failure. I have nothing to offer you."

For a moment she rested her head on my neck. "My darling, you're a loving husband and father, and a family can walk a long way on love." She sniffed my face and then licked the salty wetness on my cheek. "I think you're sad because you're tired. We all slept, but you had a stressful day. Spinnaker, can you smell wild blackberries? Let's stop here until the dawn comes."

I was so full of misery that I wanted to argue with her, but she was right, and there was a thicket of wild blackberries on the other side of the road. In the dark, we sniffed out some ripe berries and then rested under the bushes in a spot untouched by rain. I knew the thorns that surrounded us would provide protection from any stray dog or cat. I closed my eyes.

When I opened them again, it was daylight and my back was against a nest of prickles. I moved, and the prickles moved. I rolled over and saw—a hedgehog. Oh my goodness! I had been sleeping back to back with a large brown hedgehog, who was now looking at me with kindly curiosity. "So you're awake then?"

She had such a thick country accent that I barely understood the words. "What are you doing here?" I asked, but as soon as I said it, I realised it was a silly question. I also knew what the answer would be.

"I live here," she said.

"This is your home?" I looked around the underside of the thorny bush. There was no sign of the family and Roger, but I could hear them on the other side, picking fruit. "I didn't know this was your nest. I'm very sorry."

"Don't be," she said. "Plenty of room." She turned her head towards a rustling noise. "They're eating the thingummies on the whatchamacallit."

"Blackberries," I said.

"Yes, those thingummies." She put her head on one side. "City rat?"

"No, I'm a Ship rat, but I come from the city."

She nodded. "Taking your family to Ratenburg, eh?"

I was surprised. "How do you know?"

The hedgehog snuffled a small laugh. "Why else would you be here? Bottomless whatsit next?"

"Bog. Yes, it is. How far is it?"

"On the other side of the ghost trees. Big swamp with lots of whoflicky! You must be very careful."

"What is the—" I tried to remember the word "—flicky thing?"

"The whoflicky? Mud. Very sucky mud. You step off the solid thingy and it pulls you down." She shuffled closer until her eye was close to mine. "There's solid thingy and not-solid thingy. Lumps of grass. You need to know the difference. Stick is the answer. Take a stick. Poke, poke. Solid grass, good. Floating grass, goodbye."

"Madam, I'm so grateful for that advice. We were told the Bottomless Bog was dangerous, but no one said what that danger was. Is there anything else we need to know?"

"Whoflicky," she said. "Just whoflicky." That appeared to be the end of the conversation, because she turned and waddled away through the brambles, and she did not look back. She had given me valuable advice.

I could hear squeaks of pleasure as my family feasted on blackberries. What had the hedgehog called them? Thingummies! But I needed to tell the ratlets to be quiet. We were not out of dog country yet.

The morning was clear and misty, the sun not yet up and raindrops lay as silver balls in the creases of leaves. There was scarcely a ripe berry and all the ratlets, and Roger, had stained fur about their mouths. Retsina ate more delicately but her front paw pads were dark red with juice.

"We should live in the country, Papa!" Beta said. "There's so much to eat!"

And so much to eat us, I thought. I stood on my hind legs to reach a dark blackberry that promised sweetness. "Have you heard any dogs?"

"No," Beta said. "It might be too early."

"Make sure they don't hear us," I told them. The blackberry fell with a small plop and I took it in my mouth.

Roger smiled at me. "That would go down well with a drop of milk."

"Yes, Roger. And good morning to you, too." I looked past him to Gamma, who was trying to stand on his front paws to flick ripe blackberries off a branch with the tip of his tail. "Gamma, I need to talk to you about the swamp."

"Why, Papa?"

I smiled. My dear athletic son could be forgetful. "Because the Bottomless Bog is in your map memory, Gamma. And I have some more information to add to it."

The ghost trees mentioned by the hedgehog were a cluster of poplars that had died. Bare branches reached upwards, pale grey, not a leaf in sight. At this point, the road ceased, its end marked by white-painted barriers and red signs warning cars to go no further. I was surprised that cars could read these signs, but Roger assured me that motor transport was very intelligent these days. We stopped at the barrier, aware of other signs that showed humming beans sinking in water. I knew it was not water that lay ahead, but sticky whoflicky, mud that could suck us down to bottomless depths.

"That can't be true," said Delta. "Nothing is bottomless."

"This bog is," Gamma insisted.

Delta's whiskers curled. "If it's bottomless then it must be a hole right through to the other side of the planet, in which case the water would drain out."

"It's called the Bottomless Bog." Gamma emphasised each word.

"Names are not necessarily accurate," Delta replied. "Everything on this earth has a bottom."

At this, Beta and Alpha giggled. They danced and sang, "I've got a bottom. You've got a bottom. Everything's got a bottom."

"Girls!" said Retsina. "Hush! This is very important. Listen to Papa and Gamma. They have worked out a plan for crossing this swamp."

I said, "We get over the bog by walking on clumps of grass. The problem is this: some of the grass is on solid ground, other clumps are floating. If we tread on the floating islands, they will sink beneath us. But all the clumps look the same."

Beta, now frightened, asked, "So how do we get across?"

"I will go first," I told her. "I will walk two-paw like a humming bean, and I will carry a strong stick to poke each lump of grass before I tread on it. You will follow. None of you will step onto grass I haven't tested. Is that clear?"

They said yes, but I asked them individually to repeat my instructions. I wanted to be sure they all understood the importance of obeying orders. Only when I was certain did I lead them to the other side of the white barrier.

The bog could not have been bottomless because there were many more dead trees ahead, different kinds, some of which I recognised—willow, gum, poplar, oak. The sun shone on a surface that looked like water, but as we got closer, we realised it was black mud, gleaming like coal. Sticking out of the mud were tussocks, mostly green grass but also some small shrubs and buttercups. My stick was a thin branch of yew with the leaves torn off. I chose yew because although it is not a pleasant wood, being toxic to taste, it is strong, and I knew it would not break halfway across the swamp. I gave the family my last order: "Follow me—and stay together!"

The first five grass clumps were solid, and the way seemed easier than I had imagined; it was a simple matter to jump from one to another. But when I poked my stick at the sixth, a lump of short grass growing in a tangle of watercress, the little island wobbled and tipped sideways like a sinking boat. The dark mud around it gurgled, sending up bubbles that popped with a stagnant smell. I felt quite faint. After five solid clumps I had grown so confident that I was ready to forget about my stick. I looked back at the ratlets and tried my best to sound cheerful. "That one's a bad egg—and it smells like it." I turned sideways, poked another lump. Yes, it was solid. "We'll have to make a short detour," I said.

After that, I was very careful. There were only a few floating grasses, but it was impossible to know them by sight alone. I was so pleased I had the hedgehog's advice. Without it, we would have been sunk. The memory of the milking shed was still fresh in my mind, and having escaped certain death in white milk I was not anxious to risk it in black mud. The prodding stick was a valuable guide, although we soon discovered we could not go in a straight line across the swamp. Sometimes, we needed to go back in order to find a different route on stable grass clumps. It was a slow and difficult journey. Some of the ratlets were impatient.

"Papa, you listened to a hedgehog," Gamma said. "Hedgehogs are heavy. Rats are light. We could jump one at a time onto a floating island, and I'm sure it wouldn't sink. If it did tip, I would just jump off again."

"We won't risk it, Gamma. If you fall in the mud, that's it. No one can rescue you." I poked my stick at some grass and it wobbled, sending out thick ripples. We had to go back again.

On one of the stable islands, I put a stone in my mouth. It was very small, a mere pebble. When I had the ratlets' attention, I spat the stone at the mud. As light as it was, it hit the mud with a glop and immediately sank, leaving a small hole that closed over. I didn't have to say anything. The lesson was obvious. They all shivered, and Retsina said severely, "Gamma, this is your map memory! I expect you to be responsible and do what is safe. Obey your father!"

Gamma laughed. "I was only thinking out loud."

For once, Jolly Roger supported me. "Don't be such a mouse!" he said to Gamma. "We're not here to take risks."

So we continued, testing each clump of grass before we jumped. The sky had clouded. It hung like a grey roof propped up by dead trees, and I thought we might have rain again. I was anxious to get across the swamp before more wetness came, for I had no idea how a downpour would affect the mud level in Bottomless Bog. But I could not hasten our journey. Dying in this foul-smelling ooze would be much worse than drowning in milk.

Dear friend, I would like to tell you that we got through the bog unscathed, but we didn't. It was careful, practical Delta who fell in. We don't know how it happened. The gap between the two green islands was not great. Even Beta, the smallest, jumped it with ease. I can only assume that Delta had jumped absent-mindedly. I turned when Retsina gave a horrified squeak, and saw poor Delta clutching grass with mouth and claws, while his lower half was submerged in that dark, sucking mud. I yelled at the others, "Hold him! Pull him out!"

Retsina and the other three ratlets were now with Delta but there was more panic than progress, and Delta had freed his mouth to shout, "Don't leave me! Don't let me sink!"

I handed my stick to Jolly Roger, "Hold this! Don't lose it!" and went back through the weeds to Delta. He had stopped calling out, and again had his teeth fastened around grass stalks that would surely give way as the mud sucked him down. I needed to act quickly. One of us could not pull him out. We all had to do it. It would have to be a team tail tow.

I looked into Delta's frightened eyes. "Listen carefully, my son. We're going to get you out. We're lining up, jaw to tail—your brother, sisters, your mother and then me. When I say the word I want you to let go of the weeds and grab my tail. See it? There's a bump near the end. Whatever you do, don't bite that bump. Hold onto it higher up and don't let go. Do you understand? Don't hold onto the broken bit!"

He nodded, and that slight movement rippled the thick mud around his hind legs.

I positioned myself so that my tail was close to his mouth, then I made sure that Retsina's elegant tail was close to mine. "Is everyone ready? All right, Delta. Now!"

He let go of the grass and, immediately, the mud sucked him back. As a result, his jaws closed on the bump on my tail. Oh, the pain of it! I would have screamed had my jaws not been clamped to Retsina's tail. She was holding onto Beta, Beta to Gamma and Gamma had the tail of Alpha, who was out in front. Without a word, we all pulled. We all heard the sucking sound, and smelled the foul mud, as slowly, very slowly, Delta came out onto the green island. Poor Delta. He looked as though he had been dipped in tar. He lay on the grass, gasping and shaking with fright.

I cautiously curled my tail about me to examine it. There was no feeling in the end of it, and I could see the reason why. The lump was hanging by a sliver of skin to the rest of the tail. When I licked it, it dropped off. Yes, right off! I had lost a whisker's length of tail. It lay on the ground like a small dead worm with a lumpy head, and I knew that I would be like those rats who've had their tails caught in humming-bean traps.

Retsina saw it. "Oh Spinnaker," she whispered, nuzzling my cheek. "What a great sacrifice you have made for our son."

That made me feel better. Yes, I suppose it was a sacrifice, although to tell the truth, the end of my tail had been useless after that train guard's boot. But I liked the thought that I had given part of myself to save Delta.

The other ratlets came back to see their brother safely out of the bog. "You smell awful!" said Alpha.

Beta comforted him. "Don't try to lick your fur, Delta. That horrible mud could still kill you. It might be poisonous. Wait until we find a stream."

Gamma patted Delta on the head. "Brother, we defeated the undefeatable bottomless bog." Then he looked at me and his eyes went wide. "Papa! Your tail!"

Retsina leaned against me. "Your father's tail has always been handsome. Now it is both handsome and brave."

I laughed and swished my tail. "Short is very fashionable," I said.

"Did I show you the tooth marks in my tail?" said Jolly Roger, ready to retell the story of the milk.

Alpha cut in. "Uncle Roger helped us, Papa. I held on to his tail when we pulled Delta out of the mud."

Roger was pleased with himself. "I had to make my contribution," he said.

I looked at him. "Where is the stick?"

"The stick?"

"Yes! The poking stick. I told you to hold it. Don't lose it, I said."

"Yes, yes, I know." Roger looked in the grass. "It's here

somewhere. I dropped it when I needed to rescue Gamma."
He parted some tall weeds. "It can't have walked."

"Maybe it flew," I said.

"Flew?"

"Maybe you didn't drop it. Maybe you tossed it and it landed in the mud."

"I would never do that!" But now Roger looked uncomfortable, for clearly, the yew stick was not on the island.

I, too, was feeling great discomfort, and I am not talking about my amputated tail end. Without that yew stick we had nothing to test solid ground in the stretch of bog that remained. We were marooned.

Soon everyone realised the gravity of our situation. Roger made a series of jittery excuses. He had laid the stick carefully in the grass and someone had kicked it over the side. He had given the stick to Alpha. Or was it Gamma? The grass was wet and the stick was slippery. None of this was his fault.

Delta was standing and shaking himself, trying to get rid of the mud that coated the lower half of his body. The others helped Roger to look again in the grass. They trampled the island as flat as a tablecloth. There was no stick.

Gamma stood up on his hind paws and stretched. "At the risk of making myself unpopular, I have a suggestion."

"Any suggestion would be welcome," I told him.

"See that dead tree? The one with grass around it? I think I can jump that far."

The tree he indicated was a small oak some distance away. The branches spread wide and there were a few dried leaves on some limbs almost above us. On the near side of the bottom of the trunk was an island of short grass and twigs. I said, "Gamma, of this I am certain: that island is a floater. It will tip you into the mud."

"I'm fast," said Gamma. "I will be up that tree in the shake of a whisker. I can chew through a branch, drop it down to you and then jump down myself."

I could see logic in his suggestion but was afraid for him. That first jump was four rats long, a colossal leap even for an athlete like Gamma. If he did land near the trunk, it was likely he would go through the mat of weed, or else it would tip him into the bog. "I'm sorry, Gamma. It's brave of you to offer, but I can't allow it. We'll wait. Maybe someone will come by to help us?"

"Who?" asked Gamma.

No one answered him.

"I would run," said Gamma. "Like this!"

I thought he was merely demonstrating how he could run across the solid land beneath us, but then I saw that his speed was increasing.

"Gamma!" Retsina called in fright.

That reckless ratlet left the edge of our island and

sailed through the air, ears flattened, tail straight behind him. Over the mud he went, like a bird. Then, nearer the tree, he brought his hind legs up under his chest. I saw what he intended. He landed feet first on the grass mat and in the same movement launched himself at the tree trunk. Just as well, for the clump of weed and twigs split in two and sank into the mud.

"Well done, Gamma!" called Alpha.

My brave, disobedient son had his claws embedded in the bark. He grinned at us, and then scuttled up the tree as though this was something he had done every day of his life. Chewing through a thin, straight branch took a little longer. He nibbled carefully, his legs and tail wrapped around a thicker branch, higher up. We watched as his sharp little teeth worked through the wood. At one stage he paused to say the wood was still damp and strong. "It won't break when you poke the islands."

Eventually the branch sagged, tearing some of the remaining fibres. "Step back!" Gamma yelled. We moved away as he bent over to deliver a few more bites, the last done with a toss of his head that propelled the stick our way. It fell neatly beside me and I was able to nip off some protruding twigs.

Gamma went as far as he could on the overhanging branch. "Now you'll have to catch me!" he called.

At once, Retsina and Roger and I stood on our hind

legs. We made a triangle and held our front paws together in the middle. "Jump!" I shouted.

We didn't catch him as we intended, but we did break his fall, and he got to his feet, as sprightly as ever. I tested the stick. It was even better than the first, being a little longer. I reached out and prodded the next green mass. Yes, it was firm. We would get across the bog before the rain came.

The rest of the journey went without incident. The only tension was between my two sons who, after their perilous adventures, could only go back to their old argument as to whether the bog was bottomless or not.

When we came to the other side, the clouds released their burden and we walked some distance through thick grass that dripped with water. At one place the water had filled a small hollow. Retsina told Delta to sit in it.

"But it's cold," he said.

Retsina was firm. "I don't care if the bog is bottomless or not. You are going to have a bogless bottom."

With that, dear friend, we left the smell of that foul bog behind us.

CHAPTER SEVEN

A LAND OF ENEMIES AND FRIENDS

Delta is sensible about everything. He quickly recovered from his terrifying experience, and refused to talk about it, would not even explain why his jump had failed to land him on solid land. As soon as the mud was washed off his haunches, he busied himself planning the next phase of the trip that was in his memory. "Hawks are day hunters," he said.

"What if the blue-tailed song hawks are different?" asked Alpha.

"Do you know of any bird that sings at night?" he said.

"Yes," said Alpha. "Owls."

"Hawks are not owls."

Retsina intervened. "Is this going to be another silly argument?"

"No argument," replied Delta. "I am right. Cats and owls are dangerous at night. Hawks and dogs hunt during the day. We are half a day from the Forest of Perilous Pines, so I suggest we rest tonight and travel again in the morning. When we get to the forest, we'll go into hiding until it is dark again."

That seemed a reasonable plan. We were still in the weed wilderness near the end of Bottomless Bog. The sun was low, and although there were still dead trees in the area, the ground was solid. We would need to find shelter before dark.

Retsina found a hollow in a dead tree. It was dry and comfortable, apart from a few spiders that Jolly Roger ate. I shuddered when I saw spiders' legs at the corner of his mouth. Arachnids were not a part of my diet. The rest of us fossicked for grass seeds, which were plentiful, although dry and tasteless, then we curled up among the cobwebs and as usual the ratlets clamoured for a story.

Retsina repeated the tale about her brother's love of fruit and how he stole her black olive because he thought it was a grape. That started everyone talking about their favourite food. The ratlets listed such delicacies as peanuts, bacon rind, pizza crust and cornflakes. Jolly old Roger's eyes gleamed. "I know what Spinny's favourite food is."

I waited for it.

"Milk!" he said.

No one laughed. I said to him, "Apart from unfortunate spiders, what do you like to eat?"

He did not react to my sarcasm, but smiled and rolled his eyes upwards as though a memory was hanging above his head. "Popcorn!" he exclaimed. "When the theatre was empty, we'd go between the seats and pick up delicious kernels of popcorn—puffy, salty, buttery..." He got lost in the memory and saliva dribbled at the corner of his mouth.

"So you were a Theatre rat," I said with some satisfaction. "I always thought you were a bit of an actor."

"It was a movie theatre, shipmate. Films. Only for a short time, though. You know how it is. You go from place to place until you get the boot. My clan is definitely Pirate rat, yo ho ho and a bottle of rum." He scratched himself. "The food wasn't good at sea, salt pork and hard ship's biscuit. Boring, I have to say. The projection room of the picture theatre offered more. I still have a great fondness for popcorn."

I sniffed. Salt pork and ship's biscuit indeed! That was a thousand generations back in Pirate rat history. He was making it up. The movie theatre was probably make-believe, too. Who was this Jolly Roger who had attached himself to my family? Was he some lonely rat without friends? Was he a trickster or, worse, a criminal? Could we trust him? While he gabbled on about popcorn, my head was full of questions and concern for my family. The more I thought about it, the more my whiskers twitched, telling me there was some something I did not know. Some comfort came with darkness, for there, in a gap of clear sky opposite the tree hole, was our beautiful family star. I alerted Retsina and the ratlets and they crowded around me to gaze at it. How lovely it was, a lamp of reassurance. Retsina rested her head against me, and I whispered to our young, "Our very own star! See how steady its light is!"

From the back of the tree hole came a grunt and a terse voice said, "It's the planet Venus."

Arrogant mouse! I thought.

We settled to sleep and woke the next morning to a clear, cloudless day. After more grass seeds softened by sips of dew, we planned our direction by the sun, Delta assuring us that it would be midday before we came to the edge of the Forest of Perilous Pines and the hawks' territory. In the earth, Delta scratched some lines that represented his memory of the map. "We are here. Between us and the pine forest is land covered with vegetation, bushes, grasses, a few stony areas. Uncle Signal said there were no humming beans."

"That means no cats and dogs," said Beta.

"Unless there are wild cats," said Delta. "But it should be quite safe. Today, we won't go any further than here." He pointed to a line outside a circle. "This is the last stretch of wilderness before the Forest of Perilous Pines. The problem with pines is that nothing grows under them. There's only a mat of needles. So once we're there, we'll have no hiding place if the hawks attack. We have to travel when it's dark."

We were ready. Although my tail was shorter than it had been the morning before, it was less painful. The crushed area had caused me constant soreness, and now that the lumpy part had come off, I was not nearly so uncomfortable. Retsina and I walked as we usually did, with the ratlets in a line between us, but this time I went in front and Retsina walked at the back. "You shouldn't risk another attack on your tail," she said.

Roger, as usual, walked in the group where he pleased, but more often than not, he was by my side. He chattered a lot, mainly to draw attention to himself, and I thought he was probably a very lonely rat. My opinion of him became more generous. The sun was warm on our backs, the earth smelled sweet and it was surprising how a mood changed when pain eased.

There were animal tracks in the long grass, and the scent of deer and wild pigs, sometimes faint and some-times fresh. I also caught a whiff of ducks and decided there was probably a pond nearby—nests in the reeds, eggs in the nests. Thoughts of duck eggs were a great temptation. But I knew an angry duck would not hesitate to attack a small rat and so we kept moving. I sighed. The responsibilities of parenthood could be a nuisance.

By mid-morning, the earth under our paws was less soft, more stony, and the growth was not so thick. By standing on my hind legs, I could see over the stubby weeds. There was more of the same barren land ahead, mounds of stone and rock dotted with dry plants, and an occasional small tree. I suggested that we rest under one of these shrubs until the day was over.

Delta objected. "We're still a long way from the forest."

"There's very little cover," I said.

"Cover isn't needed when there's no danger," Delta patiently explained. "Sniff the air, Papa. Sniff the ground.

What can you smell? Beetles, mice, some ground birds. We should walk until middle-day. By then we'll be tired. We'll sleep and go through the pines when it's dark."

My sensible son was right about the smells around us, so we continued the journey, although my whiskers were trembling slightly. Where Delta had made a mistake was in his calculation of the habitat of blue-tailed song hawks. They may have had their nests in the Forest of Perilous Pines, but their aerial territory was much wider. Also, a bird of prey flying high leaves no scent on the land.

Fortunately for us, my whiskers are reliable. They suddenly shook so violently that I yelled, "Follow me! Run!" and we raced across some open ground to the small hill of rocks and stones. No sooner had we reached it than the sky seemed to fill with sound. I would not have called it a song. It went up and down over many notes but it was harsh, more like a scream. I looked up and saw, hovering above us, a huge bird. It had a blue tail. It also had a great curved beak and talons curved to snatch a meal.

Retsina saw it and pushed the ratlets into the narrow cleft between two rocks. We crowded in after them, but there was not much room. The bird could not swoop down and grab us in its claws, but that was not going to stop it. It landed on the rock, folded its wings and screeched in a menacing manner. I looked up. Its head was on one side as it stared back at me with a red eye.

The smell of musty feathers was powerful. Its beak opened, and in a lightning movement, it struck at the place where I was crouched next to Gamma. The beak hit the rock above my head. The bird pulled its head back and eyed me again. Then it shifted forward on its massive claws. I saw the dark feathers on its breast and belly, the bright colour of its tail. I pushed Gamma down into the cleft and stood over him. My teeth were bared but I knew my bite would be no match for the hawk's beak.

As I prepared for the attack, I heard a small, unfamiliar squeak. "In here! In here!" I looked down and saw Roger and three ratlets wriggling through a hole at the base of the rock. Gamma followed and I dropped down as the bird struck again. Once more its beak hit the rock face, missing me by a whisker. I looked for Retsina. She wasn't there. As the bird came over the crevice, I, too, wriggled into the hole. It was a tight fit around my stomach and haunches, but I made it, and heard a furious shriek behind me. The hawk had lost its lunch.

In front of me were Roger and my family, so for a while I didn't know who had saved us from the bird. But I should have known from the pitch of the squeak. The small cave in the rock was occupied by three mice.

Let me tell you this, dear friend, generally rats and mice do not get on well together. We compete for the same territory, the same food supply, but the differences are more substantial than that. I would have to say that, overall, rats despise mice. One of the worst insults a rat can offer another rat is to call him or her a mouse. Mice, on the other hand, are contemptuous of rats, seeing them as rogues and bullies. Although we are distant relations, the gulf between us is so wide that I have always considered it impossible to cross. Which is why I was amazed that these small field mice should come to our aid.

The older mouse, a squat-nosed creature, introduced himself as Moonshine, and he wasted no time in berating us in a shrill voice: "You're pathetic, that's what you are. I've seen more brains in a potato."

Delta said, "Potatoes don't have—" But I nudged him.

"Why would you be gallivanting around hawk country in broad daylight? Is it your mission to become part of a hawk? You near as dammit did just that!"

Retsina clasped her two front paws. "Thank you, thank you, Moonshine Mouse. We were mistaken. We were told the hawks were in the Forest of Perilous Pines."

"So you didn't think they could fly, huh?"

We looked at each other and didn't say anything. This small, angry mouse made us sound and feel rather stupid. I decided it was time to introduce myself.

"I am Spinnaker of the Ship rat clan. This is Retsina, my wife, and our children, Alpha, Beta, Gamma and Delta."

Roger bowed low. "I am Jolly Roger of the bold tradition of Pirate rats. Pleased to meet you, Moonshine."

Moonshine, however, had turned his attention back to Retsina. "What did you say your name is?"

"Retsina."

"Ah!" His expression changed and he looked at her with admiration. "Retsina! Now that's a fine name. I believe I feel a poem coming on." He cleared his throat. "Moonshine's all about whisky. Retsina's all about wine. Welcome, my fine rattess. I think we'll get on fine." As small as he was, he then came close to my wife and touched her nose with his in a manner I did not like one little bit. I would have bitten the insolent creature, had he not sheltered us from the ferocious hawk. Then I thought how ridiculous that was. If he had not got us away from the hawk, I would not be alive to bite him—or anyone else.

Moonshine then squeaked at the two young mice and they scurried away down a passage to get us food and drink. The food, dragged in on large leaves, was very good: ripe hawthorn berries, mushrooms, hazelnuts and some pieces of honeycomb. The drink, though, presented in acorn cups, was disgusting. He said it was made from flower nectar but that was hard to believe, for it burned the mouth more than the worst of humming-bean liquor. The only one of us able to sip it was Roger, who became

increasingly jolly as he finished one acorn cup and moved on to another. He and the mouse sang together, songs made up by Moonshine, who fancied himself a poet.

Most of the songs were extremely silly, and in favour of Retsina, who ignored them. Now don't misunderstand me, dear friend. My beautiful wife is often admired by male rats, to whom she reacts calmly, kindly and with dignity. But an elderly mouse one third her size? I believe the songs embarrassed her, for she moved to the far side of the nest and gathered the ratlets around her, making sure they did not drink from the acorn cups. The intoxicated mouse must have realised what she was doing, but he took this as a challenge and squeaked all the louder. "I couldn't be keener, on lovely Retsina..."

As for the two young mice who served us, they didn't say a word, although we tried several times to engage them in conversation. Perhaps they were afraid. Maybe they'd been taught never to speak to rats. As soon as they'd presented us with food, they would scuttle away down the little dark hole.

I nibbled on a hazelnut and reflected on the ups and downs of the last few days. It was extraordinary that we should be targeted as food by a blue-tailed song hawk, and in the next instant, find ourselves being fed by a drunken, singing mouse. There appeared to be some connection, but I didn't know what that was. The hazelnut was delicious.

Moonshine and Roger were on their hind legs and singing a new song. "Going to Ratenburg, the city of rats. Ain't got no dogs. Ain't got no cats. And if old Ratenburg falls down, we'll take a trip to Mousie town." When they finished, Roger leaned against Moonshine, who fell over and stayed on the ground, sound asleep. Roger looked at him in a puzzled way, then went down on all fours, and moved towards a full acorn cup. He didn't get there. He also rolled over and went to sleep.

Although we had not drunk the horrible stuff, we too were tired. We went to the far side of the mouse burrow and curled up as family, Retsina and I forming a semicircle, with the ratlets snuggled against us. In the moment before I drifted into sleep, I listened to our soft breathing, six rats, each a slightly different sound, but all in harmony and rhythm. I thought it was the most beautiful sound on earth.

Moonshine woke us to tell us the sun had set and the hawks would be back in their nests. The old mouse looked sober, although his eyes still sparkled at Retsina. I held my tongue because he was trying to be helpful.

Delta asked him, "Please, how far is it to the Forest of Perilous Pines?"

"You'll be there by midnight," said Moonshine. "Stony ground most of the way. Two small streams to cross, shallow, not swift. You'll be all right holding tails. Before dawn get a hiding place in the forest. Those blasted hawks wake up at first light."

I said, "We were told there's no hiding place in the forest."

Moonshine snorted. "Who said that piffle? 'Course there's places. Look for the biggest pines, roots sticking out of the ground. Dig under the roots. Stay there. Don't go out to stretch your legs. It'll be the last thing you do. Those blasted birds see everything and they dive faster than the wind. Stay hidden till night comes. See these two?" He jerked his head towards the young mice behind him. "They were caught, one in each talon. Another bird came. Hawk fight. These two were dropped and I dragged them inside. Haven't said a word since. Shock, you see. Lucky they didn't lose more than their voices."

The two young mice turned away, heads down, and set to work, tidying the burrow.

I thanked Moonshine most sincerely. He was an odd character, to be sure, but beneath some annoying traits, he was generous. I could understand a mouse rescuing a couple of young mice, but a family of rats? That showed a certain greatness of heart, and I was sorry I had been less than charitable in my opinions of him. Mind you, when he clasped Retsina around the neck and sang a final goodbye in her ear, my sorrow lessened.

He said to us, "When you're out of the pine forest, my

friend Barker will give you a paw. I'll send him a message by dragonfly to look out for you."

"Thanks," I said, although I was much amused. Barker! What a name for a mouse. It was almost as odd as Moonshine.

He guided us out into the cleft of the rock, and then beyond to open sky and land. Immediately I saw our family star overhead, but I didn't remark on it, to avoid comment from Roger. We said farewell to Moonshine, thanked him again and started walking towards the pine forest over a wilderness of gravel and small plants.

Roger was quiet much of the way, because he had an aching head, but at one stage, he paid Moonshine a compliment. "There are mice and there are mice," he said. "That mouse deserves to be called a rat."

I didn't say anything. I had already decided that prejudice came from ignorance.

CHAPTER EIGHT

A DAY IN THE FOREST OF PERILOUS PINES

Moonshine was right. The dark towers of pine trees came before us in the middle of the night, and the ground beneath our paws changed in texture, stone replaced by the rustling smoothness of dried pine needles. The forest was so dense that we could no longer see the starry sky. In the tops of those dark trees were nests where savage predators had their eyes closed until dawn. Before then, we needed to be hidden.

As soon as we entered the forest, I was looking for tall old trees with gnarled roots above the ground. My night-sight was good for nearness, but I found it difficult to see distant objects. Our daughter Alpha had excellent farsightedness in the dark and she directed us to several trees that had possibilities. Their big roots arched over the bed of pine needles, but the earth beneath was too stony and hard for easy digging. As the night progressed, I became increasingly anxious. I could not see the sky to the east. How would we know the coming of day? In the end, it was Delta who came up with a solution: "Papa, the ground is too hard to dig one big hole. Why don't we make three small ones?"

That seemed to me to be infinitely reasonable. We selected one big tree that had roots splayed out in all directions, and chose the three roots that offered the best protection. We all took turns at digging, scratching out dry clay and small stones to form a cave long enough to avoid a hawk's neck and beak.

Delta, always practical, considered the bird's anatomy. "Blue-tailed song hawks are predators that hunt from the air. Their beaks and talons are not made for scratching and digging. As long as we're out of reach, we'll be safe."

Night in the forest was still densely black when we completed the three burrows, lining them with pine needles for comfort. I still had no idea of how close we were to dawn, but I suggested that now was a good time to move into shelter. Retsina decided that an adult rat should be in each hole. I agreed, and suggested that Alpha and Beta go with their mother. I sent Delta to keep Roger company, because I knew my son would keep Roger from any foolish decisions. Gamma would come with me.

I felt uneasy at being separated from Retsina and the other ratlets, but thought we'd been wise in making three separate nests. Gamma settled in beside me and offered me his opinions about Ratenburg. "Papa, remember you said that if something was easy, it wasn't worth having?"

"Did I say that?"

"Yes, and I'm convinced you're right. The way to Ratenburg is meant to be hard. We all thought that the dangers would finish after the swing bridge near the mountain. Why would we think that? Surely, the mountain will be just as difficult as the rest." His voice sounded earnest and old.

"What makes you come to that conclusion, Gamma?"

"Because that's the whole point of Ratenburg. It's the perfect city and it's only for perfect rats. That doesn't sound good, I know. No one is perfect. But it's something to be aimed at. Don't you see, Papa? Only the strongest, bravest and fittest rats get to Ratenburg. That's why the way is full of danger. It's meant to test us."

I smiled. "What about Uncle Roger? He crossed the lake of eels in a picnic basket."

I felt Gamma shrug his shoulders. "Maybe Uncle Roger won't make it. But our family will. I'm sure we'll get there."

"You go on thinking that, Gamma, and we'll all arrive triumphantly at Ratenburg. As for Jolly Roger, maybe the city needs a rat who always finds an easy way to do things. Have you thought of that?"

Gamma made no reply, although I was sure there was an answer in his head.

By now there was some grey light seeping through the entrance to our hollow, and it wasn't long before we heard the so-called song of the blue-tailed hawks. Unlike the songs of any other birds, it was a succession of harsh cries designed to freeze the heart of any ground creature. We didn't know how close the birds were, and didn't talk in case we were heard. Their cries echoed back and forth, accompanied by the whirring of wings and the occasional thump that I guessed was a heavy landing. I checked the entrance to our hollow. The space between tree root and stone was high enough for a rat crawling on its belly, but would not admit anything larger. So it was with the other two caves. We were all safe as long as no one went outside.

The scent of pine resin was strong, covering other

smells, so our noses did not detect the approach of the hawk. We didn't know it had discovered us until the light went out in our burrow, as a curved beak plugged the opening. I was reminded of the dog that had tried to scratch the rabbit burrow in Sweet Clover Meadows. The hawk would not get any further. It couldn't even see us. But it knew we were there.

Gamma pressed himself against the back wall when he saw a beak much larger than his entire body.

I said to the beak, "Go away!"

There was a ruffling of feathers, a futile movement, as the hawk struggled to get further into the hole.

"You're wasting your time," I said.

A wheezing sound came from the beak, then a surprisingly deep voice said, "I don't talk to my food."

"We are not your food," I replied.

"You are rats," said the beak. "All rats are food. Having a conversation with dinner is a great waste of time."

"You're a stupid bird," I said. "And we'll never be your dinner. So please remove your beak from our entrance."

"Or we will push your beak out," said Gamma, who was now behind me.

"Oh-oh! A little one!" The beak opened wider and I saw a short, pointed tongue. "You are small and weak. Your puny body has no strength. You could not push a fly if it landed on your nose."

I felt Gamma quiver and grabbed him just in time. "Do you know what would happen if you went near that beak?" I whispered.

He shrank back, aware that he had nearly walked into a trap.

"Come on, little one!" coaxed the hawk. "If you can move my beak, I will go away and leave you in peace."

"You mean pieces," said Gamma from the back of the burrow.

The bird grunted and then gave a sigh. "I told you there is no point in talking to food."

I wondered if hawks had discovered the other two burrows and had pushed in their beaks in a similar way. It occurred to me that most rats going through the forest found shelter under tree roots, and the hawks knew this. They had probably developed techniques for prising us out of our holes. I wondered what the bird would do next. It didn't do anything. It didn't need to do anything. It was blocking the entrance and, therefore, our air supply. The air grew stale, putrid with the bird's breath.

"It's getting stuffy in here," said Gamma.

"So it is!" said the beak. "Do you need to come out for air?"

I whispered in Gamma's ear, "Say yes."

He turned to me in the dark.

I grabbed his ear again. "Say yes, but don't move."

Gamma called to the beak, "Yes, I'd like to come out for fresh air."

"Oh good!" the hawk replied. "I'll move to one side, and you can get past me."

The beak came out of the hole. Light and fresh pine-scented air came in. We saw curved claws on a scaly foot and knew the hawk was ready to pounce. The foot twitched. "Are you coming?"

"No," said Gamma.

"You said you needed to come out for air," said the hawk, its voice still coaxing.

"We've got air, thank you," I said.

There was an angry growl, and the beak plunged us into darkness again. "Typical rats!" it said.

"You told us it was a waste of time talking to food," said Gamma, with amusement in his voice.

I didn't want to get too close to the beak, but I realised the hawk's nostrils were set on top, and inside the hole. This meant that the bird was breathing the same air as us, and like us, knew when the atmosphere was becoming suffocating. The theory proved correct. When Gamma and I were next feeling uncomfortable, the hawk withdrew its beak and pretended that it was leaving us. Air flowed in, but the musty feather smell was still outside the burrow and we knew the bird was waiting to pounce.

The day dragged on. The hawk was stupid but persistent and towards dusk either hunger or weariness caused it to fly away. When its odour had gone, Gamma wanted us to visit the other two caves, but I insisted that we stay in our shelter until the forest was dark. Both Signal and Moonshine had assured us that night was safe. Even then, I was cautious leaving our cave. We discovered the others were still in their shelters, waiting for us. No, they said, there had been no visit from a hawk. I found it odd they weren't discovered, but Delta had an explanation. "The birds probably check out every tree. They thought all the rat smell at our tree came from you and Gamma."

He could have been right, or perhaps the others had simply been lucky. They'd had a tense day, however, listening to the hawk's cries, and they were as anxious as Gamma and I to get out of the pine forest. So although we were hungry and thirsty, we took no detours, but walked in a straight line, following the trail that Delta had set by the stars. We did not see our family star, for it was low on the horizon and blocked by massive trees. But I knew it was there. We travelled in silence, paws making an occasional rustling sound on the loose pine needles, ears and noses alert for danger.

The smell of hawks was all around us, mixed with the scent of tree resin. I was nervous, wondering if all blue-tailed song hawks slept at night. Were there exceptions? What kind of night-sight did they have? And what of owls, who were definitely night predators? We had not seen or smelled other birds in the area, but it was possible an owl could fly in from outside. I was constantly aware that we had no sheltering undergrowth, should we be suddenly attacked. My only reassurance came from my whiskers, which were quite still.

Well before dawn we came out of the forest and found ourselves under a huge arch of stars that included a pale, claw-shaped moon. The pine needles had gone and we were on stony ground with small plants.

"There's our star!" said Retsina, her whiskers touching my neck.

"Venus," grunted Roger.

We took no notice of him. "It was always with us, my darling," I murmured. "We couldn't see it for the trees, but it was there, waiting and watching over us."

She tenderly licked behind my ear. "Oh Spinnaker, you are so wise. I know you'll get us to Ratenburg."

I felt the warmth of her breath on my face. "My dear,

I would take you to the end of the earth, if that's where you wanted to go."

She snuggled against me. "Ratenburg will do," she said.

The stony ground changed to soft earth containing a variety of taller weeds and some evidence of humming-bean habitation. We passed through a fence made of rusted strands of wire and wooden posts covered with lichen. Further on was a humming-bean house, all its windows blind and unseeing, and its doors shut. We sniffed. The scent of humming beans was faint, as was the odour of cat, chickens, mice and bees. In the porch lay some leather boot-skins and a pillow-lined cane basket, both surrounded by dead leaves and dust. The place certainly looked empty and safe.

Roger, in his search for fresh water, had discovered a dripping tap by a garden that contained, of all things, a row of sweetcorn. We could not believe our good fortune. It seemed a lifetime since our last meal of corn. I sighed with pleasure. We had come through the forest unscathed and here, waiting for us, was a feast of food and drink. Gamma scampered up a stalk and bit off a fat corncob. It fell with a delicious thud.

Near the dripping tap was a large metal container, lying on its side. I recognised it from a memory of the time my father Mizzen, my brother Hawser and I lived in a house with a garden. It was a watering can. I looked at the sky, now dark grey. "Day is near," I said. "Hawks may come this far. We know that is possible. I suggest we eat where we can't be seen from the sky. Let's roll the corncob into this watering can."

Alpha, Delta and Gamma rolled the corn and we followed. There was a small amount of moisture inside the can, but that didn't concern us. The corn was in peak condition and we were hungry. With three on one side of the cob and four on the other, we quickly bit through the soft wrapping and into kernels that spurted sweet juice. We were so busy eating that we didn't notice a movement at the open end of the watering can. Only when Alpha gave a terrified squeak did I look behind me.

What I saw made me choke with fear. This was worse than the encounter with the hawk. Oh, oh, oh! Why had I led my family into this inescapable prison?

In front of the watering can, a very large tabby cat was smiling at us.

CHAPTER NINE

WHAT IS BAD IS GOOD,
AND WHAT IS GOOD IS BAD

Dear friend, I have been in danger many times, and have managed to escape by skill or luck. This time I knew I would have to die for my family. The cat could cope with only one rat at a time, and that rat would be me. If I could manage to struggle before I was eaten, the cat would be sufficiently occupied that the others could run past us. I took a last fond look at my darling wife and children, even gave Roger a farewell glance. Then I walked towards the cat.

It was a big animal with green eyes and sharp teeth in its smile. It could afford to look relaxed. It had us trapped. I came closer to those fat grey paws, and I looked up at striped legs, the paler fur on its chest, expecting it to be the last thing I would see. Still, it didn't move. I looked up further. It had put its head on one side and was studying me, maybe wondering which part of me it would eat first. I was determined to die with dignity. I stood on my hind legs. "I am Spinnaker of the Ship rat clan."

The cat's smile grew wider. "How do you do," he said. "My name is Barker."

Barker? I dropped onto all four paws. Barker! I knew that name.

"You have made excellent time," said the cat. "Only moments ago, I had a dragonfly message from Moonshine."

I was so confused I could not make so much as a squeak. We had all thought that Moonshine's friend was another mouse.

The cat went on, "It's my understanding that you're on your way to Ratenburg. Moonshine sometimes refers travellers to me with the request that I act as guide and mentor in the town. Oh! You look rather embarrassed. I apologise if I'm intruding."

"You're a cat!" I exclaimed.

He gave a purring laugh. "Barker is an unusual name for a cat. I often have to explain it to visitors. Do you want to hear?"

I nodded, aware that Retsina had crept to my side.

"I live with two nice people," said the cat. "The husband wanted a dog called Barker. The wife wanted a cat. They decided to toss a coin, and a most curious thing happened. The coin landed on its edge. So they settled for a large cat called Barker.

"The woman told me I had one important duty. 'Take care of the rats and mice,' she said, and I did. I've been taking good care of them, from that day."

I'd had some bad experiences with cats, but this creature was different. He was quite relaxed and his claws were hidden. My heart stopped racing and I asked, "How long have you known Moonshine?"

"Ages, dear fellow. We're both getting quite grey in the whiskers. He likes to help travellers at his end, and I do my best here. There is, you know, a little stream of rats going to Ratenburg."

"We haven't seen any other rats," said Retsina.

"Is this your dear lady?" asked the cat.

"Yes, this is my wife Retsina."

"Charmed to meet you," said the cat. "Well, these days it's not so much a stream of rats as a trickle. The dangers on the way appear to have increased, which is why we endeavour to do our best." He waved a paw. "Are these your children?"

A head came up from behind the corncob. "Not me, shipmate," said Jolly Roger, who had been out of sight. "I'm from the Pirate rat clan and a friend of the family."

Beta came forward, staying close to me and her mother. "We thought you'd come to eat us," she said to Barker.

The cat shuddered. "Oh, my goodness, no! What a horrible suggestion! No offence, my dear, but I'm a vegetarian. Speaking of which, did I interrupt your breakfast? I'm terribly sorry."

"We'd almost finished," said Retsina. "We were about to go out to drink from the tap."

Barker flicked his striped tail. "The tap? One drop at a time? That is so tedious. Come with me and I'll offer you my drinking bowl—full of fresh water."

We followed him around the corner of the house, where a pottery bowl sat on a platform of bricks, near a herb garden. I could smell sage and mint, but the smell of cat was stronger and I wasn't entirely comfortable drinking from cat-tainted water. I remembered, however, my earlier prejudice about mice, and while I still believed that cats were usually enemies, I was prepared to see Barker as an exception. He really did take care of us.

He told us that the town of Grissenden was intensely ratophobic. "The people blame rats for every misfortune. If a child gets a cold, it's caused by rats. If milk turns sour? Rats again. I knew of a woman whose car had a puncture, and she said rats must have chewed her tyre."

"That's absurd," I said. "Why would a rat want to bite a car tyre?"

Barker waved a paw. "It wouldn't. But that's the problem with phobias. When something goes wrong, people look for someone to blame. They don't care if their accusations are unjust and illogical. They still do it. In Grissenden, the victims are rats and mice."

"Are you saying it's not safe to go through the town?" I said, wondering if it would be possible to go around it.

"Oh goodness, I know what you're thinking. You really do have to go through the town. There's the sea on one side of it, and a nasty big river on the other. I wouldn't recommend either. What I'm saying, my friends, is that you must observe a few rules. Number one is walk at the edge of the main highway. Cats and dogs aren't permitted on that road, and you can be sure motorists aren't going to get out of their cars when they see some rats. They'll simply go home and write a letter to the paper. Rule number two is never eat anything. The most delicious morsels are laid out in tempting places, and all are poisonous."

"Including vegetables?" Retsina asked in a quivering voice.

"Not here, my lovely," said Barker. "You can eat anything here. My employers grow excellent corn, as you have discovered. I'm talking about poison in the town of Grissenden." He looked at the ratlets. "Tell me, little sprogs, what is rule number two?"

"Never eat anything in Grissenden," they chanted.

Barker purred. "One hundred per cent correct. Now for rule number three. Never, never go near a trap. Grissenden traps are fiendishly clever, and they are everywhere my dearie-os. Big traps, small traps, traps that look like rat shelters, traps that look like smiling mouths. Rule number four is beware of cheese."

"Cheese?" Jolly Roger's jaw dropped. A slice of cheddar was his favourite meal.

"Yes indeed! Cheesy-weesy! The people of Grissenden have made rat-catching a highly developed sport, and they now have a cheese known as REC. That stands for Rat Effective Cheese. It's highly aromatic, and many rats find it irresistible. For the sake of your dear ratty lives, avoid cheese."

"All cheese?" asked Roger.

"Absolutely all cheese." Barker blinked at the Pirate rat. "But if you were obeying rule number two, you would not be thinking of cheese. Is that not so?"

"Of course," said Roger in a businesslike voice. "My question was merely for the benefit of these young rats, who might be misled."

I looked at him. He was an impossible liar.

Retsina, who was claiming the memory map for Grissenden, went through the list. "One, walk at edge of main highway. Two, eat no food. Three, avoid traps. Four, ignore all cheese." She paused. "Thank you, Barker. That is very helpful. How far is it to Grissenden?"

"You'll come to the highway by high sun, and you'll be through the town before darkness. You need have no fear of hawks in Grissenden. Too many hawks were caught in rat traps. What a how-de-do! Feathers all over the place! Now they avoid the town like the plague. Occasionally, we see a blue-tailed song hawk here, but don't worry, my darlings. I will go with you as far as the town. Once you're on the highway, you'll be safe as long as you obey the rules."

I found it incredible that a cat could be so helpful. "You are very kind," I said.

Barker waved a paw. "Think nothing of it, dearie-o. It's my job to take care of rats and mice."

For most of the early morning, we walked through farmland, Barker beside us. As I've already mentioned, he was a big cat, almost the size of a dog. Only once did we see a hawk, and it was a mere speck in the sky. Barker took no chances. "They have eyes like telescopes," he said, and he made us all stand beneath his body. I needed to explain to the ratlets what a telescope was, but at the same time, I was looking around me at a grey and white furry roof supported by four strong fur pillars. If the hawk did see us, it would not dare attack.

Near one farm, we passed a curly black dog that would have come after us, had it not been for Barker. The two knew each other. "A fine morning to you, Barker," called the dog, while greedily watching us. "Doing your good deed for the day, are you?"

"Nice to see you in such good health, Towser," Barker meowed. "How did you like those vege dog crackers I gave you?"

The dog's expression answered that question, and it turned away, its tail curled between its hind legs.

Barker smiled at us. "Don't mind Towser. If his teeth and stomach were as good as his heart, he'd be a remarkably fine dog."

Near the outskirts of the town, the cat led us to a small stream where we could drink again. "Fill yourselves. It's a hot day. There's nothing worse than dying of thirst and seeing a fancy bowl of poisoned water. Remember, from here on through the town, your pretty mouths are only for talking."

It was time to say goodbye to Barker. I had a speech prepared, about the guidance of our family star and how it had brought us amazing help in unexpected ways, from a hedgehog, a mouse and a cat. I wanted to talk a little about the importance of this journey and how these three creatures had given up all their selfish instincts to help us on our way to Ratenburg. I stood on my hind paws and looked up at Barker. "I would like to say—"

He interrupted. "It's my job. Goodbye, my dearie-os." And with that, he ran off, his long legs stretching over the grass, like those of a galloping horse.

Again, we formed a walking line, the ratlets between me and their mother, and Jolly Roger somewhere in between, next to whoever would provide an ear for his fantastic stories.

A small rise took us onto the highway, where there was a considerable amount of traffic. Not that we went on the road. We travelled in the vegetation at the edge and sometimes needed to cross patches of short grass. The humming beans who roared past in cars must have seen us, but, as Barker had predicted, no one stopped. Each vehicle caused a wind that ruffled our fur, while the big trucks, thundering by at speed, caused a gale that tangled our whiskers and sometimes knocked us off our feet.

In one patch of cut grass we passed a few ripe cherries, shining in the sun, although there was no cherry tree nearby. Further on, there was an intact meat pie resting against a thistle bush.

"These foods are so obviously poisonous baits!" said Alpha, pointing at the crust untouched by birds or insects.

I addressed my children. "Ratlets, let this be a lesson to us all. The cherries and pie look most appetising, and the only reason we know they're toxic is because we had a warning from a charitable cat. Let us also be charitable. We should not tell ourselves that all cats are bad. There are some notable exceptions—like Barker."

Beta said, "Most rats think cats are bad. I suppose grasshoppers think all rats are bad."

"Grasshoppers?" Gamma frowned.

"We eat grasshoppers," said Beta. "They must hate us."

"For goodness' sake, Beta!" Gamma cried. "Grasshoppers are different. They're made to be eaten."

"They are insects," said Beta. "They are living creatures and they have feelings."

136

Before Gamma could retort, Delta said, "Beta's right. The relationship between cats and rats is the same as that between rats and grasshoppers."

"It isn't," said Delta. "I don't eat grasshoppers." He thumped his tail against the ground. "They're greatly overrated, all crunch and no taste. Give me a fresh sparrow egg, any day."

Retsina stepped between Beta and her sons. "I don't like all this talk about food," she said sternly.

"We were only thinking out loud," protested Gamma.

I agreed with my wife. "Thinking about food leads to talking about it and talking leads to eating. If you want to employ your minds, think of something worthwhile. Focus on Ratenburg."

We continued along the edge of the highway. On either side, beyond the strips of vegetation, were high metal fences, mesh big enough for rats, but not of a size to admit cats and dogs. Through the fences, we glimpsed more roads lined with humming bean houses.

Barker's number one rule, walk along the highway, was not difficult if we also obeyed the other rules. The only time we had to walk on paved road was at the turn-offs, side roads that went down to the town. There were not many of those. The main danger came from the baits, which looked very appetising.

"Here's another one!" shouted Alpha. "Chocolates!"

On the grass, a square of gold paper presented two dark chocolates that had not melted with the sun. A few steps on, there was a small mound of sugar-frosted cookies.

I realised it was impossible not to think of food when we were passing the kind of meals we dreamed about. The ratlets were fascinated. I could see saliva shining on Beta's whiskers. "Listen!" I said. "We will take note of these baits. How many are there? Let us count the number of times we could have died."

That worked. Their fascination turned to dread as the tally rose: a ham sandwich, a bag of peanuts, two hard-boiled eggs, some potato chips, a whole rasher of cooked bacon. Now each item represented a dead rat.

The baits seemed fewer as we neared the other side of the town, but here we found a new danger. Retsina, who was walking in front, suddenly dropped out of sight.

"Mama!" the ratlets screamed.

My dear wife was unharmed, but if she had been on her own, she would have been trapped in a metal-lined hole in the ground. The ratophobic humming beans had dug the hole, lined it with some tin pipe and placed grass straws over the top. She had fallen through.

She was more annoyed than upset. "May a thousand fleas infest their armpits!" she said, stamping her paws. "May their teeth fall into their porridge!"

It was easy to pull her out. We employed the same

rat-tail tow that we had used to get Delta out of the bog, but this time there was no sucking mud to hold her back. Retsina came up the side, spitting crumbs of dirt and angry words. "Do they call that a sophisticated trap?" she said.

"Watch where you step," I called to the others. "If you can't see earth, there probably isn't any."

Later we saw another hole, just as carefully disguised, grass stalks on top looking like mown hay. I poked the edge, and the stalks fell into the deep, slippery pit. How fortunate we were to be a family, I thought. A single rat travelling this road, without family and friends, would not get far.

It seemed that poison baits had been replaced by traps, but near the end of the road, a special scent hung in the air, something so tantalising and delicious that it had to be the REC of Barker's last warning. I had never smelled anything like it. It was as though all my wishes for cheese had come true and moulded themselves into one flavour. My nose and whiskers trembled. Saliva ran down my fur. Every one of us was affected, and Jolly Roger was making tiny squeaks as though he was in agony.

Yes, my friend, it was cheese, but oh, what cheese! That smell drove us mad. We hurried, following the thickening of that wonderful aroma, and saw in front of us a huge trap. Set well back from the road, between some small bushes and the high mesh fence, it was simply a big version of an old-fashioned mousetrap. It had a spring holding a steel bar that would be released when the bait was touched. The bait, of course, was a slab of that special REC. Rat Effective Cheese!

"Come away, ratlets," I called.

"Wait," said Roger. "This bait isn't poisonous."

"How do you know?" I asked.

He pointed. "Look at those ants." He indicated three black ants that were removing crumbs of cheese. "It's logical, shipmate. They don't put poison bait in a trap. Why would they? You can't kill something twice."

"Stay back, Roger," I warned. "It's big and it's deadly."

"It's also got the best cheese in the world—and the ants are eating it!" Roger jumped up and down. "Spinny, me lad, I know traps. I can release this and the cheese will be ours."

My whiskers were dancing on my face, but I could not find fault with Roger's argument, so I supposed it was simply the marvellous smell that was making my face hair mobile. I watched while Jolly old Roger gnawed a stalk off a fennel bush. He dragged it across to the trap. "Stand back, everyone!"

We all stepped back a pace.

Roger eased the fennel stalk over the wooden base of the trap, while we all held our breath. He pushed it

further in, touched the spring, and slam! The metal bar came down, crushing the stick and making the trap lift off the ground. Roger gave a cry of delight, and as soon as the trap settled, he ran forward to collect that lump of REC. "You are mine!" he yelled.

At the same time, Retsina shouted, "Stop!" and she grabbed Roger's tail. She yanked it so hard that he turned a backward somersault, landing on the ground as a second metal bar, nearer the cheese, thudded down with great force. Roger sat on the ground, staring at near death.

The ratlets walked backwards, and so did I. The cheese was probably now safe, but we had lost our appetites. Roger didn't complain about Retsina grabbing his wounded tail. Indeed, he didn't say anything. Head down, and slightly wobbly, he walked away from the trap, and we all travelled in silence out of the town of Grissenden.

CHAPTER TEN

MEANINGFUL FICTION AND MEANINGLESS TRUTH

When Roger rushed for the cheese, Retsina had acted instinctively to save him. Later, she told me she had surprised herself. "I've grown used to him," she said. "He's become a part of the family."

I had to admit that I was greatly relieved when she pulled him away from danger. Many a time I had wished that Jolly old Roger would disappear, but the thought of him lying on a trap, with a neck broken by a steel bar, brought a wave of sadness. He was lazy, greedy and unreliable, but Retsina was right. If he had been killed, we would have felt considerable loss.

Roger, being Roger, changed the story. Once he'd recovered from his fright, he denied trying to get at the REC bait. "I knew the second spring was there," he said. "I simply wanted to know how that horrible trap worked."

Alpha reminded him that he had said, "You are mine!" to the cheese.

"Wrong on two counts," he told Alpha. "I said, 'You are mean,' and I said it to the trap, not the bait."

Arguing with him was of no use whatsoever: he had more excuses than a fish has scales. Because we were silent, he thought he'd convinced us, and he walked jauntily, telling us what a lovely day it was—as if we didn't know.

We were on the same road, but beyond Grissenden it had ceased to be a highway and was narrower, with only occasional traffic. There were no mesh fences and we had some clear views of farmland with cows and pigs, and humming beans sitting on earth machines. Ahead, the road was even smaller. It went over a hill, looking like a string over a green parcel of land. Even further in the distance, as misty as cloud, was a mountain range.

"Stop!" I commanded, and everyone turned to me. "Look ahead! What do you see?"

"A hill," said Beta. "Some trees."

"Yes, yes, but in the distance! What is it?"

"Some mountains?" suggested Gamma.

Retsina knew. She came close to me and her beautiful eyes were bright as she stared into our future.

"I see a road that goes on forever," growled Roger. "Isn't it time we stopped for a rest?"

I looked at our ratlets and said, "Tell them, Retsina."

She smiled. "They're not some mountains. They are *the* mountains. On the other side of them is a valley—" She paused.

Beta's eyes opened wide. "Ratenburg?"

"Yes, Ratenburg."

Our young squeaked and cheered, and even Roger did a small dance of excitement. We all stood on our back paws, stretching to see better, but the mountain range was far distant and only visible because the day was clear.

I said to the family, "Roger's right. We need to rest now. There are trees near the top of that hill. They should provide safe shelter."

We knew we were nearing the end of the Railway rats' map, but actually seeing the mountains filled us with new energy. I'm sure, dear friend, that we would have kept on walking, such was our enthusiasm. I have also learned that every positive feeling has a negative side, and too much enthusiasm can make creatures careless, especially if their senses have been dulled with weariness. We had walked much of the day as well as the previous night, and it was time to catch up with ourselves. As we travelled up the hill, our views were wider. We saw a great stretch of water far to the left, and a fast-flowing river to our right, exactly as Moonshine Mouse had described. I thought the river was probably the same one that went under the swing bridge near the mountain. Compared with the perils we had already met, a rope-and-plank bridge did not seem such a dangerous thing.

The trees at the top of the hill proved to be a grove of willows next to a small road that led to a farmhouse. I had hoped for apple or plum trees, but the willows would give us shelter, and we could fossick for a meal after dark. Then Roger drew attention to a box on a post by the gate.

"This is it!" he said. "The perfect hiding place!"

I looked up at the white-painted box. It had a gap in the front, not large, but wide enough to be an entrance. I was doubtful. "I've seen boxes like this in the city."

"That's right," said Roger. "They're birdhouses. People make them for birds to nest in. Funny world, isn't it, shipmate? The two-legs hate rats but they love birds. Many a day I've had breakfast on bread thrown out for sparrows."

I sniffed the post but could detect no bird odour. "Are you certain these things are birdhouses?"

"Absolutely," said Roger. "I once found a couple of starlings in one. They thought I was after their eggs—bad-tempered pair."

I was certain he had been egg hunting, just as I was sure there were no birds in this box. It was of a size that could accommodate us all.

"Darling, I think we should shelter in the trees," Retsina said.

"Cats can climb trees," said Roger. "No cats or dogs can get us in a birdhouse. That's why they are made this way."

"I'll investigate," I told my anxious wife. I ran up the pole, eased myself over the platform and peered through the gap in the box. It was empty, except for some paper on the floor. "No one's home!" I called cheerfully. "Come on up!"

One by one, they followed me: Roger, Gamma, Beta, Alpha, Delta and finally Retsina. For once, Roger was right. It was an admirable shelter. The papers lining the floor of the box provided a soft nest, and we were very comfortable. I lay at the front so I could see through the gap, and the others curled in a heap behind me. They were all asleep in minutes and I, too, was dozing when I heard the crunch of heavy steps on gravel. Instantly,

147

I was alert. The smell of humming bean was strong, yet when I looked through the gap, no one was there. Someone must have passed by on the road. The footsteps stopped. I heard humming-bean breathing, snorting sounds and then an extraordinary thing happened. The back wall of the birdhouse fell open. I jumped, and everyone woke up. The back wall had gone! How could this have happened?

But wait, dear friend, it gets worse. A face filled the open space, and what a face it was! Round eyes behind glass windows, red cheeks with little blue lines in them and a thin red mouth! The eyes stared and then the mouth opened. A scream came out, louder than a song from a blue-tailed hawk. None of us could move.

"Rats! Filthy rats!"

The back wall of the box slammed into place and we heard rapid crunching noises as the humming bean ran away.

Roger lay down again. "That scared her off," he said.

"No, it didn't," I said. "She's probably gone to get her cat. Or a gun. We have to get out of here before she returns."

Haste made us clumsy, and we were slower getting out of the birdhouse than we were climbing in. I helped the ratlets and Retsina through the gap, then turned to Roger, who still insisted that the humming bean would not come back.

"All right," I said. "You can stay here on your own." But as I put my head through the opening, Roger decided to move. Unfortunately, he tried to push himself through at the narrowest end of the gap, and he was caught around the middle.

I was now outside the box and on the platform. Below me, Retsina and the ratlets were running towards the willow trees. I said to Roger, "That end is too small. Go back and come through down here."

He waved his front paws at me. "I can't! I tried but I'm stuck. Help me!"

The last squeak sounded urgent because we could both hear the barking of a dog. "Try harder!" I said, as I glanced at the ground. My sensible Retsina had reached the trunk of a willow and was ushering our young up it.

The barking of the dog was getting louder, and the female humming bean was screaming encouragement "Get 'em! Get 'em, boy!" The number of feet on the gravel road was now six instead of two.

"Help me!" screamed Roger.

There was only one way to do this. I climbed back inside the box and went to the far wall. Then I ran as fast as I could and hurled myself at Roger's rear end. He shot out so fast that he flew through the air, missed the platform and fell to the ground. I climbed out and looked down. He was sitting on the grass, looking dazed.

The humming bean and her big cattle dog were almost at the gate. She was screaming. "Get those filthy rats!"

I scampered down the pole and pushed Roger into action. "Dog!" I said.

We took off as the creature broke out of the gate. Lucky for us, the humming bean had him on a lead. The dog was straining to get after Roger and me, but it was being dragged towards the box on the pole. "Get those stinking rats!" she yelled, and she opened the back wall of the box. The dog wasn't looking at the box. It was jumping up and down on the end of its lead, watching me and Roger, and barking terrible language at us. When the humming bean saw the box was empty, she let the dog loose, but by then it was too late. We were climbing up the nearest willow tree, aiming for a high branch.

I knew that Retsina and the ratlets were several trees away, but I couldn't get to them. Roger, frightened and sore, crouched beside me in the fork of a branch, while below, the dog lay in the grass by the trunk, looking up and growling. "Stupid rats! You'll come down sooner or later. I'll sit here all today and all night and all next week if I have to. I've got a lot of patience."

Roger groaned softly.

The dog went on. "You rats have the brains of blow-flies. What made you move into the old lady's letter box?"

I looked at Roger. He pretended not to notice.

"Right on mail collection time, too. How stupid is that?"

I felt Roger move as though he was going to say something to the dog, and I stopped him. "Don't answer him. If we refuse to speak to him, he might get bored and go away."

"It's better to be chased by a dog than a cat," Roger said. "Dogs don't climb trees."

"So I'm meant to be grateful?" I was angry with him, not only because I had believed his idiotic birdhouse theory, but also because he'd got himself stuck and I, once again, was separated from my family. "Roger, I'm sick and tired of your tall stories."

He stuck his chin out. "What tall stories?"

"Birdhouse! Huh!"

"It was the same shape as a birdhouse."

"See? There you go again. One excuse after another! You wouldn't know the truth if it bit you on the backside," I hissed in his ear.

"You're the liar," he said. "You're always picking on me like I'm a waste of space."

"Because you are lazy and greedy!"

"I've saved your life twice and this is how you thank me!"

"Once," I said. "You pulled me out of the milk pot and I pushed you out of a letter box. That makes us even."

"Twice," he insisted.

"The first time you stole my ratlets' food and I chased you out of the building. That doesn't count."

He wasn't going to give in. "I didn't steal their food. I took it so you would run after me, and I could get you out of the building."

"Rubbish! That's something else you invented." I was so angry now, I couldn't stop. "This Pirate rat business. It's sheer fantasy! The way you go around with your shiver me timbers and your yo ho ho! Everyone knows you're making it up."

"And everyone knows you're a pompous bully," he squealed. "You think you're the big rat king."

There was a stirring under the tree and the dog barked, "What's going on up there?"

I leaned back against the rough willow bark. This idiot rat had gone too far. I hissed, "I do my best to look after my family!"

"You preach at them," he said. "You give them orders."

"I do not!"

"You do! And you're mean. You treat me like a mouse."

I took a deep breath. It was useless talking to someone who thought only of himself. "If that's how you feel, then you may leave us."

"I will," he sniffed. "As soon as I get down from this tree. No respectable Pirate rat would tolerate this nonsense." He glared at me. "Be glad that I don't have a sword."

He sounded so ridiculous that I laughed. "Oh, stop acting, you pathetic fool! Your name isn't Jolly Roger!"

He stared at me, his mouth hanging open. He looked as though I had suddenly hit him on the snout.

Before he could invent another lie, I put the evidence to him. "The Jolly Roger is the skull and crossbones flag flown by pirate ships—a thousand generations ago. We all know that. Your Pirate background exists only in your head!"

I expected a bunch of blustering stories, but there was silence. After a while he said in a sulky voice, "You pretend you're better than me. You're not. I'm from the same clan as you. My parents were Ship rats. They gave me a terrible name so I changed it. There's nothing wrong with that."

This sounded like the beginning of another tall tale. "What's your real name?" I demanded.

"It's the name of a ship's flag. I only changed it to another flag. Jolly Roger was more interesting."

I repeated my question. "What—is—your—real—name?"

"Ensign," he said.

I realised he had damp fur. The silly rat was crying! I said, "What's wrong with that? A lot of Ship rats are called Ensign."

He sniffed. "I'm the only one I know."

I looked at him carefully. "Roger, who is your father?"

"Was," said Roger. "He's dead. Killed in a humming-bean raid. Mum and us ratlets escaped."

"And your mother's name?"

"Pools."

"Pools?"

"That's right." He sniffed again. "Mum moved us into a nest behind the wall of a food factory. It was very embarrassing."

"A food factory!" I believed that this, at last, was the truth. "There's nothing wrong with living in a food factory! Why did you make up those stories about pirates?"

He was quiet for a moment, then he said, "It was a dog-food factory."

I laughed and laughed. It doesn't seem amusing now but then it was very funny, especially with that big cattle dog lying under our tree. Of course, Roger didn't know what I found hilarious, so I said through gasps, "This—this tree is a dog-food factory!"

"And we are the dog food!" said Roger with a little giggle. Then we were both laughing as though everything in the world was a big joke.

There was a loud growl from below and a fresh wave of dog smell came to us.

"You'll stop laughing when I bite your heads off."

That made us laugh all the more, and by the time we

were exhausted, the dog was also tired. We heard soft, grunting snores as regular as a heartbeat. It was asleep. We discussed the possibility of leaving our tree and joining Retsina and the ratlets in their willow, perhaps all escaping down the road, before it woke up. But we decided not to risk movement. If the creature was a light sleeper we would truly be dog meat.

The sky darkened. I crept to a higher branch, hoping to see the tree that housed my family. What I did see was the next best thing: our star low in the sky, shining hope for the future.

"Venus," said a voice. Roger had followed me. He, too, had his nose pointed to the sky. "You know it's the planet Venus. Why do you insist on calling it a star?"

"Because that's what it means to us. Words must have meaning. Roger, I think I understand why you changed your name. It wasn't because Ensign was terrible. It's actually a very nice name. But it had no meaning for you. If you like, I shall continue to call you Jolly Roger."

"Thank you." There was a pause. "That still hasn't answered my question. I know what Venus means to you and your family, but why call it a star?"

"Do you know your letters?"

"Most of them."

"Then what is star backwards?"

"Oh. Rats. I see." His eyes glowed in the dark. "Like my mum."

I stared at him. "Your mother Pools?"

"That's right," he said. "After Dad died, she changed her name too. Backwards like your star."

My heart beat so fast, I thought it would explode and shatter my ribs. "Roger, I'm going to ask you something. This is very, very important, so tell me the truth. Do you remember your father's name?"

"Of course I do! That was another terrible name. It was Mizzen!"

CHAPTER ELEVEN

THE BRIDGE TO THE LAND OF DREAMS

Dear friend, can you imagine the shock? Jolly Roger, our ex-neighbour and current fellow traveller, was my brother! I felt as though the breath had gone out of me. I nearly fell off the branch.

We forgot the dog at the base of the tree, even forgot about Ratenburg, as we compared memories. As I said earlier, my father Mizzen, my brother Hawser and I escaped when the humming-bean pest control company killed wharf rats. We hoped my mother Sloop and the rest of the family had got away, but when we found no trace of them, we thought they must have died. Hawser and I were very young at the time, but of course I remembered my brother Ensign. He was a quiet little rat, unexceptional in looks and personality. In my memory, his only distinguishing quality was a love of food. He was always hungry. I did not recognise my timid brother Ensign in this large, flamboyant Jolly Roger.

Roger was squeaking with excitement at our discovery. "I thought I was the only one left!" His paws were on me as he licked my nose.

I was very moved, although I found his affection excessive. "I had the same thought," I replied. "When our father and Hawser disappeared, I was sure I was a solitary orphan."

"Is that why your family is so important to you?" Roger asked.

I was silent, for his words went deep inside me. Finally, I said, "Yes, I suppose it is."

He too, was quiet for a while. "I'm your family," he said.

I touched his neck with my paw. "Yes, Roger. You're my family. You are part of us." I sincerely meant it, although I did wonder what the ratlets would say when I told them that Uncle Roger was truly their uncle.

A beam of light moved down the path from the house. Behind it was the woman with the window eyes, a torch in one hand, a dog lead in the other. The hound by our tree woke up and barked, "Leave me here! I'll get them when they come down."

But humming beans don't understand creature language. "Come on, Hunter. They're gone now. Time to go home."

The dog's barking grew louder. "They haven't gone, you stupid two-leg! I need to stay by the tree."

The lead was clipped onto its collar and it was pulled towards the gate.

"Good dog," she said. "Nice boy, Hunter."

"Stupid! Stupid!" it barked all the way up the path.

"It is impossible to train some humming beans," I said to Roger. "Which is just as well for us. Now we can join the rest of the family."

We ran down the tree, only to find that Retsina and the ratlets had had the same idea and come down from their willow to find us. Retsina's first words were, "What was that all about?"

"What?" I asked.

"The noise!" she said, looking from me to Roger. "Shouting! Laughing! What was going on?"

"You sounded angry, Papa," said Alpha. "Then it was a joke."

"Tell her, Spinny!" Roger could not contain himself. "Tell them what we discovered." Then he rushed in with, "Hey, you kids, I'm your uncle!"

"So?" Alpha tilted her head.

"Real uncle! Spinny is my brother!"

"Spinnaker," I said. Then I told Retsina and the young a shortened account of our family history. If Retsina and Alpha looked politely shocked, Gamma showed much interest. "Does this mean we're related to Pirate rats?"

Roger opened his mouth and closed it again. He looked at me.

"Ship rats," I told Gamma. "Historically, some Ship rats went over to pirate ships. Being a Pirate rat was a choice, but Ship rat was the name of the clan. We're definitely Ship rats."

"Different from the Restaurant rats," Retsina reminded us. She turned to Roger. "I'm glad you and Spinnaker made this discovery. You know, I always thought you two were alike."

"What?" I stared at her.

"Small likenesses," she said. "The shape of your paws and the way you're so sure of yourselves."

I couldn't believe I was hearing this from my devoted wife.

"Sure of ourselves?" Roger seemed to find this amusing. He glanced back at the letter box on the pole. "Even when we're wrong?"

"Especially when you're wrong," said Retsina, smiling. "Listen!"

We all turned our heads to take in all directions. All I could hear, apart from insects, was the distant barking of that frustrated dog.

Retsina said, "That dog isn't going to sleep. It may get loose. We shouldn't stay here, talking."

She was right. We ate a few dew-soaked grass seeds and then resumed our journey along that narrow road, down the hill and then up another rise. We were supposed to be in line, but the ratlets were crowded around Jolly Roger, who told them about life in the rafters of a dog-food factory. They seemed to find that more interesting than his pirate stories, perhaps because it came from experience and not mere imagination. Retsina and I walked together.

"We need to accept Roger as family," I told her.

"Of course," she said. "I thought we were already doing that. Now I know the reason for it."

I sighed. "You're a wonderful Restaurant rat."

"Greek restaurant," she said.

The road continued to go up, down, up, down, as did the countryside around us, and although we could not see the mountains in the dark, we knew that we were journeying through the foothills. The air was getting cooler, and from the scents that hung over the road, we guessed we were passing a mix of farmland and forest. We could smell sheep in one area, chickens in another, and on one hill the strong odour of gum trees. Once, we picked up the scent of a cat, but it was a faint smell, about two days old, and suggested no danger.

At this point, Retsina turned to me and said, "I've noticed something very peculiar."

"What, my dear?"

She leaned against me. "Think of all the creatures we have met on this journey."

"No more than usual," I said.

"We're going to Ratenburg," she said. "Yet we haven't seen another rat."

I thought about it. "Not everyone knows where Ratenburg is. They don't have the map."

She said, "I'm sure lots of rats have travelled through here. Otherwise, why would there be so much ratophobia?"

I didn't like to tell her that most rat travellers would not have got past the dangers. They would have ended up in the stomachs of giant eels, or been killed by farm dogs, drowned in a bog, snatched by hawks, poisoned and trapped. I tried to put her mind at rest. "Darling, such a hazardous journey would make most rats very cautious. I imagine they're on the road like us, but all in hiding."

"It's still very peculiar," she said.

The dirt road became smaller, a narrow walking track, and we decided to rest until dawn. Delta discovered a fallen log, hollow at one end, slightly damp and smelling of rotten wood. Inside, it was empty save for a bit of fungus. The ratlets settled down with their mother. I stayed at the entrance to keep watch for predators, and when Roger joined me, I told him to go back with the others. "Get some sleep."

"Shiver me timbers, shipmate," he said. "It's my turn to be on watch. You go and get some shut-eye."

He had fallen back into his pirate prattle, as though it were real. I wanted to feel angry with him, but then I thought what did it matter? If my brother Ensign wanted to be Jolly Roger the Pirate rat, why not let him go on pretending. "We'll both keep watch," I said.

When we came out of the log at first light, we saw a most stirring sight. In front of us was a mountain range that stretched right and left as far as we could see. In the semi-darkness the peaks looked black and forbiddingly high, and I reminded myself that we had no map for the journey up and over the top. Who lived on these slopes? Were there wild boars, hawks, hunters with guns? None of us knew what dangers were before us on this last part of the path to Ratenburg.

Around us were trees and shrubs, no sign of humming beans, which meant we could not benefit from their food stores. We were all very hungry. Roger scratched some decayed wood on the fallen log, and found several fat white grubs. The ratlets enjoyed these, but Retsina and I chose to chew on grass seeds.

We were on our way again before sun-up, although progress was slow, the track covered with sharp stones and hollows filled with water. Gamma happily ran or swam through icy-cold puddles, while his mother worried about him getting rat flu. I assumed that we were already at a high altitude because the air had a hint of frost to it.

We knew from the sound of rushing water that we were approaching the river and, eventually, we arrived at the swing bridge. I should correct that definition and say it once was a swing bridge, for now it was little more than two ropes and a few wooden boards hanging over a deep ravine. One board was ready to drop, and the others looked insecure. Obviously most of these planks had fallen into the river, and I wondered how many rats had fallen with them.

Far below, the water was a seething mass of foam around dark rocks, and merely looking down made me feel dizzy. "We'll have to walk on the rope," I said. "Which rope is the strongest?"

Retsina chose the left rope because it looked less frayed. "We'll hold tails again," she said. "Then those who slip will be held by the others."

Delta glanced down at the surging water. "We might all fall in together," he said.

"Be quiet, Delta," said Alpha.

"No arguments!" said Retsina. "You'll need your mouths for holding on. I'll go first. Alpha, you will firmly grip my tail. Beta, you'll be next. Delta, Gamma, Roger and Spinnaker, you can be at the back."

"Why is Spinny last?" cried Roger.

"Because his tail is shorter," Retsina replied.

That's how we set out on the rope, teeth gripping the tail in front, paws holding onto the rope, which was wet with spray. We tried not to look down at the foaming water, but the roar of it filled our ears. It was a monster trying to devour us.

If you have never crossed one of these bridges, my friend, please understand that they are not called swing bridges for nothing. A few steps into the gulf and the ropes shook uncontrollably. We felt helpless. Surely we would fall off into the water.

Retsina, the only one of us not gripping a tail, called, "Wrap your legs around the rope! Quickly!"

We did that, and only just in time, because the wet rope shook so much that we slid around to the underside. There we were, hanging upside down, nothing but spray between our backs and that hungry torrent of water. Retsina called out again. "I'm going to ease back to the top of the rope. Follow me! Crawl slowly and calmly. Any jerky movement will make the rope shake again."

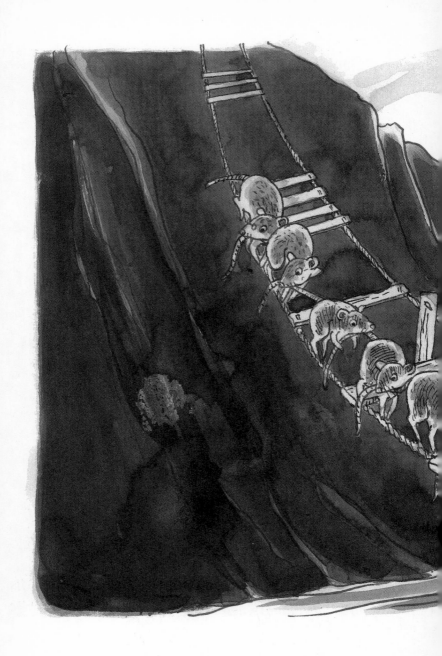

Somehow, we managed to get back with the rope under our bellies, and although it quivered and dipped, it didn't threaten to toss us off. We reached the first plank and went over it, feeling the change of texture to old wood slippery with green slime.

Retsina called encouragement but the rest of us did not dare reply. We could not relax our grip on the tail in front of us.

We had short distances between the next two planks, and the rope was quite steady, but after that there were no wooden steps, only a long loop of rope to the opposite bank.

"Be very calm," called Retsina. "Panic makes it shake. We'll go slowly, and if it does shake, we'll stop and wrap our legs around the rope, until it is still."

We didn't turn upside down again, but progress was so slow I feared that night would come and we'd all be clinging to that rope in the darkness. We did, however, get to the track on the other side, Retsina first, the rest of us following. We did not let go of the tail-tow line until we were all on rocky ground. What a crossing! We rested there for some moments, our legs still trembling from stress, our jaws and tails aching. Far below, the river thundered and we were in a fine mist of spray, but no matter. We had managed the last challenge on the Ratenburg map and there was only the mountain slope ahead. We were very pleased with ourselves. The ratlets seemed to forget their discomfort. They shook the wetness off their fur and scampered about, pushing each other and turning somersaults, as though they had actually arrived at the rat city. "We're here! We made it!"

It was late afternoon. The track wound in great curves up the side of a mountain covered with brown rocks and clumps of tussock grass. There was no shortage of adequate shelter but we would need to keep going to find food. The air was very cold, and because we were newly from the city, we had warm-weather fur, short and thin. Walking would warm us, but we also needed a nourishing meal.

There were no predators to be seen. I searched the sky for sign of hawks or hungry seabirds, and saw a solitary skylark. As for ground creatures, there were only two rabbits, who stared at us in astonishment.

Roger called to them, "We're going to Ratenburg."

They didn't answer, which did not surprise us. Rabbits do not speak to rats.

We knew they understood us, because one said, "Ratenburg!" and they both laughed in a mocking way.

When we had passed them, Retsina said, "This ground is solid rock. How do they make their burrows?"

I thought about that. "Maybe they have no enemies and don't need burrows."

Retsina shrugged. "Everything is food for something else. Of course they'll have enemies."

She was right for, further up the slope, Beta drew our attention to a wild cat running across the hillside. It had a dead rabbit in its mouth. That sight immediately brought back caution and we found a secure hiding place in a gap between two large rocks. We cleared out some pebbles, lining the space with tussock grass. By the time we had finished, mist had come down the mountain, hastening nightfall. We were all hungry, but shelter was more important than food and we tucked ourselves into the narrow crevice, huddled close to keep out the cold.

When morning came, there was still heavy mist and I had to make a decision. Did we stay in hiding or did we continue on the track? How many wild cats were there on the mountain? Did they hunt when the mountain was covered with low cloud? Would they smell us through the moist air?

"Papa, we're very hungry," said Alpha.

It was decided that Roger and I would go out and see if there was anything edible in the area. I found a nest of speckled quail eggs nearby. Roger came back through the mist, triumphant. "A thorn bush covered with berries, shipmate!"

Cautiously, we escorted Retsina and the ratlets to these discoveries and everyone had a very full breakfast.

The air was still cold but sunlight was coming through the mist, turning water drops into small rainbows. We had new energy and decided that, cats or no cats, we would continue up the mountain.

"It's not something I would recommend for a solitary traveller," I explained. "But a family of six strong rats should be able—"

"Seven!" said Roger. "A family of seven!"

"Exactly!" I corrected myself. "A family of seven rats can deter any prowling cat."

"We're an army!" said Gamma.

"We have great courage, Papa," said Alpha.

"But don't let your courage make you less cautious," I reminded her. "We will walk in line as usual, always alert for danger. A careless rat is a cat's dinner."

"You're doing it again," said Roger, licking egg yolk off a paw.

"Doing what?" I asked.

"Preaching," he said. "Spinnaker the dictator."

"Close your mouth, Roger," said Retsina. "It's making a silly noise." But she said it with a laugh, and he laughed in return.

I felt happy with the thought that, in a family, you can say what you like and feel safe. Knowing that Jolly old Roger was my brother Ensign had made a big difference. Now I understood him because he was a part of us. On top of that, there was an energy among us that brought good humour.

I ask you this, my friend: have you ever put your ear to a wall where a colony of rats are nesting? Have you heard the squeaks of newborn young and the excited chatter of proud parents, and known that you have only to gnaw a small hole to be a part of that happy gathering?

Well, that's how we felt on that mountain slope. On the other side was the place of perfection, the wonderful city of Ratenburg.

CHAPTER TWELVE

FINDING
RATENBURG

As the day went on, the mountain grew steeper and colder, until there was no vegetation on the rocky slopes, just patches of snow and ice seen through the chill mist. We didn't know how far we were from the summit. It could have been minutes away, or hours. We passed a small cave in a rock, and soon after the mist became swirling snow. That caused us to retrace our steps and return to the cave. It wasn't much of a hollow, simply a recess where some rock had fallen away, but it was big enough for seven cold rats. We crouched inside and although we were not warm, the feeling came back to our frozen paws. It was still daylight, or that murky light that passes for day, and it was story-telling time for the ratlets. They wanted Uncle Roger to tell them about his life in the dog-food factory. "What went in the dog food?" Gamma asked, although they had all heard this that same morning.

Jolly Roger put on an actor's voice. "The bones of dead horses and the blood of dead cows! The feathers of ducks! Chicken heads with staring eyes! Sacks of wheat with weevils in them!" His eyes got wilder. "Bits of old carpet! Pigeon droppings off windowsills! Dog scrapings from—"

"Roger!" said Retsina. "That's enough!"

The ratlets were laughing and burying their heads in expectation of the next line.

"Rat droppings," said Roger. "That's true, me hearties. Dogs go crazy for a nice tasty rat dropping."

"You're impossible!" Retsina said.

"I know," said Roger, winking at the ratlets, who were hugging themselves with laughter.

Our youngsters said I always told them serious stories. That is probably true. I am not my brother. But all the same, they wanted to hear about our early life under the wharf and how there was a big wave whenever a ship came alongside. "Engines work the propellers, which plough up the sea. We were on a high ledge under the wharf, but water still washed over our floor. When a big wave came we needed to hold on to the wood, or we would have been washed away."

Delta nodded. "It's called a tsunami. That's when an underwater disturbance creates a giant wave."

"Some rats were washed off the ledge," I told them. "But we were all good swimmers. There were seven ratlets in our family: five boys and two girls—me, Hawser, Ensign, Compass, Briny, Starboard and Hull."

"Did you eat fish?" Beta asked.

"Sometimes. Mostly it was whatever the humming beans threw overboard—potato peelings, cabbage, apple cores."

"Tell us about the pest control company," said Alpha.

I looked at Roger and he looked away. We had been very young, but we both remembered that dreadful day—the poisonous gases pumped under the wharves; screaming, fleeing rats, some getting away, others not able to escape. I could not talk about it. "It was just another case of ratophobia," I said.

Swirling snowflakes made a thick curtain in front of our shelter, and we were not tempted to go out. The murky light faded, became darkness, and we huddled closer as the temperature dropped. I thought sleep was impossible but when I woke there was a chink of light coming into our cave. The entrance was almost entirely blocked with snow but above it was a hint of fine day.

We dug our way out, shaking the snow off our backs, and blinked in daylight as bright as white fire. I had seen it before in the city, drifts of snow in gutters, snow packed to ice by the wheels of cars, but never had I stood before a world of undisturbed white. We huffed on our front paws, and our breath was the only mist in the day. Everything sparkled, including the eyes of our ratlets who, in spite of the cold, were enchanted with the beauty around us. Not only was the day clear and bright, we were almost at the top of the mountain.

Retsina licked my cheek. "We'll soon be home, Spinnaker," she whispered.

"Tonight we'll sleep in Ratenburg!" Roger told the ratlets.

The snow on the track was paw deep in some places, body deep in others. Being the biggest and able to push a path through drifts, I was at the front of the line. The sun rose higher and threads of steam lifted from rocks and from our fur. No one complained about the cold. We were all eager for our first glimpse of the rat city. But the view of the valley did not emerge as we expected. From below, the top of the mountain range had looked like a series of sharp peaks. In fact, the top was a rugged plateau that went as far as another horizon. The track curved over it but there was no vegetation, nothing to eat, just patches of snow and small trickles of water where that snow was melting. We were disappointed but knew we would eventually come to the place where we could look down on the valley.

My brother Roger sang, "Yo ho ho! Have a bite of snow! This mountain leads to Ratenburg town. What goes up, must come down."

I told myself that he was trying to cheer his nieces and nephews, who were cold and hungry. Unfortunately, he didn't cheer me. I wanted to thrust a pawful of snow into his mouth. Retsina sensed my agitation and turned to me. "Spinnaker dear, he's not causing any harm. This is his way of being helpful."

She was right. Roger was my brother Ensign, but he was not me. I should allow him to be himself.

By the middle of the day, the horizon had become a line of rocks in front of us, with nothing but sky beyond it. We were close to the edge. My heart beat fast and I ran towards the highest rock to be the first to see Ratenburg. The others had the same idea, and we scrambled up the rock together, crouched and leaned over the top.

The valley far below was a green basin, fields and trees, some streams as small as silver whiskers on the land. But the information we'd been given was wrong. Humming beans did live in the valley. At both ends of the basin were small villages, connected by a narrow road.

Delta was not surprised. "Logically, there must be humming beans. Otherwise, where would the food come from?"

Beta said what the rest of us were thinking. "I can't see Ratenburg."

Delta turned to her. "Why would you see it from here? Look how small the humming-bean houses are. Anyway, it's probably hidden—in that forest, or underground."

"Fear not, me hearties," said Roger. "It's there somewhere, the pot of gold at the end of the rainbow."

"Pot of gold?" Delta looked puzzled.

I said to them, "Let's go. The sooner we get out of this snow, the better."

Although the track was covered with a blanket of white, it was easy to follow, for it was flat, with rocks on either side. I realised the track would have been made by humming beans for their own use. I'd been disappointed to see their houses in the valley, but Delta was right. If there were no humming beans, where would Ratenburg get its food supplies? Was it possible there was no ratophobia in the valley?

We descended past the snow line and into an area of vegetation more varied than the tussock grass on the other side. Wild roses grew, thorny bushes close to the ground, and although the hips were withered with frost, we ate them. After that, we needed to make a decision. Did we repeat yesterday, and find early shelter on the mountain? Or did we push on down to the valley?

With their stomachs full, they all wanted to continue.

"It will be night before we get there," I warned them.

"We have no hope of finding Ratenburg in the dark," Retsina added.

Alpha said eagerly, "It'll be much easier going down the mountain than it was climbing up."

It was decided. Our shadows lengthened as the sun went down, and the air grew chill, sharp with frost. Below us, the valley turned gold with the last light of day. Our eyes strained to see Ratenburg, but in fact none of us had the faintest idea what we were looking for.

Have you ever been in that situation, dear friend? You need to find something that's very important, and yet you're not sure what it looks like? That's how we were, coming down the mountain—excited, curious, anxious.

The humming-bean houses in the village were not big by city standards. They were made of stone with tin roofs, and there were black lumps of cattle beasts grazing in the fields. We watched until the long fingers of purple shadow reached over the entire valley, and everything was in darkness.

We continued to follow the track through low hills that bore the strong scents of cows and goats. Roger moaned. "Milk!" he said. "Cream! Butter! Cheese!" In the distance, there were lights in the windows of some of the houses, and we smelled humming beans and their food. The aroma of meat and potatoes drifted across the valley to our quivering noses.

The track led us past a farmhouse and a barn with an open door. Retsina and I agreed that we needed to find a place to rest and maybe this barn was it. We stopped and sniffed the air. I could smell hay and machinery, but no cats or dogs. "Wait here," I said, "I'll make sure it's safe."

My night-sight is good, but for detail I rely on my nose. There was hay in the barn, a large tractor and tools for working the land. I called to Retsina, "Bring them in!"

After nights of cramped shelter, the size of the barn made the ratlets timid. They crept in, looking about with anxious gaze. I indicated the heap of loose hay. "It's warm and dry," I told them. "Make your own bed."

No sooner had I said it than the hay moved and out came a large rat. "What are you doing here?" she demanded.

I should have expected a rat in this valley, but I was so surprised I couldn't speak.

Retsina said, "Good evening. We're on our way to Ratenburg."

The rat was glossy and black, with eyes like bits of coal. She studied us for a moment, then turned towards the hay. "Hey, guys! Another lot of immigrants!"

At once, about twenty black rats jumped out of the hay and stood beside the first. They stared at us, neither friendly nor unfriendly, and I hastened to introduce myself. "I'm Spinnaker of the Ship rat clan and this is my wife Retsina and my children and my brother Roger. We don't wish to impose on you. All we want is shelter. We will leave at first light tomorrow."

The rat nodded. "I'm Furrow of the Farm rat clan. You came over the mountain?"

"Yes. We've travelled for several days—"

Furrow smiled at the rats beside her. "It's that old Pied Piper story again!" she said.

Retsina stepped forward. "We'd be very grateful if you let us stay the night. In the morning, you might be able to give us directions."

"Directions?"

"To Ratenburg," said Retsina.

Furrow sighed. "It's all fiddlesticks!" she said. "It's all humbug and jingle bells! How many times do I have to say this to rats like you? There's no such place as Ratenburg."

CHAPTER THIRTEEN

THE JOURNEY AND
NOT THE ARRIVAL

You may have guessed this truth, dear friend. We certainly hadn't. We were in shock. At first I thought the Farm rats were deliberately being unkind and unhelpful. In fact, they were the opposite, and Furrow, in particular, could not have been more considerate. She said, "That Ratenburg story is a myth. But a myth is not a lie, you understand. A myth is truth wrapped up in a story. You have to open up the story to find the true meaning."

Greatly upset, I shook my head. "You say Ratenburg doesn't exist. Then it's not a myth. It's an outright lie."

Furrow corrected me. "I didn't say Ratenburg doesn't exist. I said it isn't a place. The truth in the story is that Ratenburg is the journey."

"The what?"

"Ratenburg is the journey," repeated Furrow. "Most rats want a life that's easy, full of pleasure and good food. They want a Ratenburg place. But that kind of life doesn't make you strong. It doesn't teach you anything. I don't know what kind of journey you've had but I'm sure of this one thing—it was very hard work. Am I right?"

We all nodded.

"A difficult journey for nothing," said Retsina.

"Have you thought about all you've learned through those challenges?" Furrow asked.

We were silent, all bitterly disappointed. The longing for Ratenburg had made the city real to us—although I do believe if something is too good to be true, it usually isn't. But that hadn't stopped us building images of luxury in our minds.

I suspected Furrow was correct about the learning. I tried looking at our travel not as hardship but as what we had been taught on the way. We had become skilled at solving problems. We had learned a lot about ourselves, and each other. We knew what it meant to work together as a family. And I had found a brother.

The ratlets shifted and whispered to each other. I think they understood.

Retsina asked, "What happens now? When rats find out there's no rat city, where do they go?"

Furrow replied, "Some go over the mountains to new places. A few turn back. Others decide to stay in the valley. Life isn't perfect here. There are cats and dogs and farmers who hate rats. But if you've done the Ratenburg journey, you'll be okay. You've developed skills to cope with a less than perfect world."

Dear friend, we decided that we too would stay in the valley. After a while, I realised that a perfect city called Ratenburg was actually our desire to gain something better for our family. I think that on the way we found something better within us. We truly had come to a new place in our lives. I looked at the ratlets. In the future, they would have their own stories to tell their sons and daughters, who would probably become Farm rats. I sighed to think what wonderful stories would be told.

That night, while Retsina tucked our ratlets into the hay, my brother Roger and I stood in the doorway of the barn. Roger scratched his chin thoughtfully. "I wonder how many rats start out, and die before they get here."

I shook my head. "I don't know. Maybe most of them."

"Do you think they're the ones who get to Ratenburg?"

"What do you mean?"

"When they turn up their paws," said Roger. "Drop dead. They go to a perfect city for rats?"

"Maybe," I said. "And maybe not."

We were turning to go back into the barn, when he gave a sudden squeak and nudged me with a paw. "Look, Spinny! Look up there!"

I followed his gaze and saw the light in the sky.

"Our family star!" said Roger.

CHAPTER FOURTEEN

ENDINGS ARE
ALSO BEGINNINGS

It would be most ungracious of me if I were to end this story with anti-climax. To be sure there was disappointment, especially for my lovely Retsina, who had grown up with stories about the glorious city of Ratenburg. For me, disappointment was associated with exhaustion: we had given every scrap of energy to the long and difficult journey and felt betrayed by the result. It was like risking a rat trap only to discover that the cheese bait was plastic.

That first evening, I had seen logic in Furrow's wisdom, and I tried to be optimistic for the sake of my dear family, but it was several days before I truly felt gratitude. Thankfulness grew, first and foremost, for the Farm rats and their kindness. They may not have been as educated as city rats. They knew nothing of humming-bean high-rise apartments, air-conditioning ducts, buses, traffic lights, wharves and ships, and they were rather blunt in their conversations. Their hearts, however, were all goodness and they cared for a group of strangers as though we were their own.

They warned us about the farm humming beans and their cat, and told us that the pigs were friendly, having no prejudice against rats. If we ran out of food, we could visit the troughs because pigs didn't mind sharing. That made us all regret the times we had relished small slices of bacon or ham.

Then there was a baker in the village who threw out old bread and buns to the dogs. Dogs, said Furrow, preferred food from the butcher's shop. If rats waited until dark, there was always plenty of bread to be had, and sometimes a bun filled with raspberry jam and cream.

The Farm rats told us that we'd have to leave the hay shed as winter closed in, because the hay would be fed out to the cows. Then it would be best under the farmhouse, near the base of a chimney that was warm day and night.

"Bet it gets crowded," said Roger. "Bet the cat knows rats are there."

He was probably right, but we decided we had time enough to find some other winter dwelling.

Gradually we grew accustomed to country living in one place. The hardest thing for me was trusting our children to the company of young Farm rats, but, as Retsina pointed out, our babies were growing up and needed to be with rats their own age. Alpha, Beta, Gamma and Delta would come back to the hay shed, laughing, squeaking, but as soon as I tactfully enquired where they had been, they fell silent.

"Dear old Spinnaker!" Retsina nibbled my ear in that persuasive way she had. "You've been such a good papa. Go on being a good papa and don't try to hold them back."

I had to confess that this was the only shade of sadness in our new situation. My wonderful children had learned much. Now they were learning to keep secrets from me.

How could I have known so little about my family?

On the day of the first frost, Furrow told us it was time to leave the hay shed and go to winter premises. "The farmer will come with his tractor and a front-end loader. It has big prongs that are driven into the stack. The hay will be taken out in scoops and fed to the cows."

Soon after Furrow's announcement, our four ratlets and their friends rushed into the shed. Gamma jumped up and down with excitement. "Mama! Papa! Come and see what we've done!"

I can assure you, dear friend, that I had no idea what was in store for us. The youngsters took us across fields of grass coated with cold dew, over a small wooden bridge and into an overgrown orchard. There, the ground was covered with fallen leaves, yellow around the pear trees, red and brown around the cherries. On the far side was an ancient walnut tree, its branches nearly bare.

"Look up!" said one of the Farm rats.

"We've made you a house!" cried Beta.

High on the trunk was a hole as big as a large apple.

"It's hollow inside!" said Alpha. "We got rid of the spiderwebs and lined it with dry leaves. It's very cosy, Papa. It can be our winter house."

I started to climb the tree but my eyes were watery and I didn't see the sign until Alpha called, "Delta wrote that!"

Carved into the bark, above the hole, was the word *Ratenburg*.

This edition first published in 2016 by Gecko Press
PO Box 9335, Marion Square, Wellington 6141, New Zealand
info@geckopress.com

Text © Joy Cowley 2016
Illustrations © Gavin Bishop 2016
© Gecko Press Ltd 2016

All rights reserved. No part of this publication may be reproduced or transmitted
or utilised in any form, or by any means, electronic, mechanical, photocopying or
otherwise without the prior written permission of the publisher.

Distributed in New Zealand by Upstart Distribution, www.upstartpress.co.nz
Distributed in Australia by Scholastic Australia, www.scholastic.com.au
Distributed in the UK by Bounce Sales & Marketing, www.bouncemarketing.co.uk

Gecko Press acknowledges the generous support of Creative New Zealand

Cover by Vida Kelly
Edited by Anna Rogers
Text design and typesetting by Katrina Duncan
Printed in China by Everbest Printing Co. Ltd,
an accredited ISO 14001 & FSC certified printer

ISBN: 978-1-776570-75-1
Ebook available

For more curiously good books, visit www.geckopress.com